x vw.

SPECIAL MESSAGE TO READERS

ONE DARK NIGHT

Cassie Van Doren nurses a terrible secret. When she knows her end is near she sends for her niece, Selina Rochford, whom she has not seen since the girl was two. But Selina is too late: Cassie is dead. Inheriting Steeple Court, Selina sets out to find what Cassie so dreaded. Searching the cellars, she finds something appalling which has lain there for many years. But the final horror is yet to come. In the semi-darkness she sees coming towards her a woman who looks like the portrait of Aunt Cassie. A dead woman, with murder in her heart . . .

Books by Pamela Bennetts
Published by The House of Ulverscroft:

MIDSUMMER-MORNING
THE LOVING HIGHWAYMAN
RUBY
LADY OF THE MASQUE
BEAU BARRON'S LADY
LUCY'S COTTAGE

PAMELA BENNETTS

ONE DARK NIGHT

Complete and Unabridged

ULVERSCROFT
Leicester

First published in Great Britain in 1978 by
Robert Hale Limited
London

First Large Print Edition
published 2000
by arrangement with
Robert Hale Limited
London

British Library CIP Data

Bennetts, Pamela, *1922 –*
One dark night.—Large print ed.—
Ulverscroft large print series: mystery
1. Detective and mystery stories
2. Large type books
I. Title
823.9'14 [F]

ISBN 0–7089–4213–X

Published by
F. A. Thorpe (Publishing)
Anstey, Leicestershire

Set by Words & Graphics Ltd.
Anstey, Leicestershire
Printed and bound in Great Britain by
T. J. International Ltd., Padstow, Cornwall

This book is printed on acid-free paper

Acknowledgements

I am much in debt to the following authors, whose fascinating works provided me with the information I needed to write this book:

A Mysterious People
  Charles Duff.
In the Life of A Romany Gypsy
  Manfri Frederick Wood.
Gypsies of Britain
  Brian Vesey-FitzGerald.
The Victorian Underworld
  Kellow Chesney.
Madame Tussaud
  Leonard Cottrell.
Two Hundred Years of Wax Modelling — a history of Madame Tussaud's
  James Sargant.
Handbook of English Costume in the Nineteenth Century
  C. Willett Cunnington and
    Phillis Cunnington.

1

The nightmare began in a small and rather expensive hotel in Knightsbridge in the Spring of 1876. At the time, of course, I did not recognise it for what it was, and when understanding finally came to me, its tentacles were wrapped too tightly round me for escape to be possible.

I had been in London for only two weeks, and was revelling in the sights which the capital had to offer. My mother had died at my birth, and when I was two, my father had rejoined his regiment in India, taking with him his small, fretful daughter, and a lean, under-nourished girl of sixteen, called Gertrude Jennings, who was to be my nurse.

After twenty years of life on a large military post, which I am bound to confess had a number of compensations to off-set the disadvantages of heat, flies and other nuisances, my father had suddenly contracted fever, and was dead within three days.

There was nothing to keep me in India after that. Gertrude, still as thin as a bean-pole, with the same carroty hair and freckles, and just as devoted, had packed our things, arranged our passages, booked our rooms in an hotel, and reminded me firmly to write to my Aunt Cassie to tell her of my father's death, and the fact that I was on my way home.

Miss Cassandra Van Doren of Steeple Court, Leyden, in Yorkshire, was my late mother's sister. I had not seen her since I was two, and so I had no recollection of what she looked like, but we had exchanged many letters during the years, and I felt that I knew a great deal both about her, and the inhabitants of the village in which she dwelt. Cassie had a fluent pen, and her delicious descriptions of disastrous dinner-parties, and her firm opinion that the latest curate would have been more at home on the stage of a music hall than in the pulpit, had enlivened many a dull day for me.

Gertrude, who remembered my aunt quite well, said she was nothing like my mother, who had been an acknowledged beauty, but that she was a tall, dominant woman, fierce and prickly on the outside, but warmly compassionate within.

It was about four o'clock on a bright May day when Gertrude and I returned to the hotel. We had spent an ecstatic afternoon gazing at the richly filled shops in Regent

Street, marvelling at the crowds of smartly dressed Londoners, dazzled by noise, and not a little alarmed by the rush of carriages and hansom cabs which seemed bent on the destruction of any bold enough to attempt a crossing of the road.

I needed a new wardrobe, now that I was back in England, but the choice of silks and satins, fine kid boots, beaded handbags, French suede gloves and hats, to say nothing of exotic perfumes, had rather gone to my head, and finally Gertrude had risked life and limb to stop a passing carriage, bundling me and my packages into it before I could acquire yet another piece of useless frivolity.

When we reached Grey's Hotel, an obsequious clerk at the reception desk gave Gertrude our keys, snapping peremptory fingers at two page-boys and ordering them to take our parcels to our room.

We were in no hurry to mount the sweeping curve of the stairs, content to take our fill of the breath-taking dresses of the women, with their faintly rouged cheeks and lightly painted lips. The day of the bustle was over for the time being, and now the fashionable gown was slim and sheath-like in front, all the trimming and flounces at the back, ending in a small train. Colours were mixed, and spotted foulard, satin, surah, silk and velveteen were but a few of the gorgeous materials used to create society's butterflies.

Some of the women were flirting discreetly with elegant men in morning coats and tightly fitting trousers; others occupied small alcoves round the foyer, sipping China tea, and exchanging the latest gossip with their friends.

When at last we got to our room, our own tea arrived on a heavy silver tray. I was busy trying on a hat made of rose-coloured tulle and velvet, when Gertrude said quickly:

'Why, there's a letter for you, Miss Selina. Looks like Miss Van Doren's writing.'

I laughed, leaving my new bonnet on, for I thought it mightily becoming.

'It hasn't taken her long to put pen to paper. I expect she is going to warn me of the pitfalls which lie before a young woman living alone in London.'

'Or maybe the pitfalls for that same young woman if she throws her money about as if it grew on trees.'

I pulled a face as I took the letter from Gertrude.

'Don't be such a grouch, Gertie. Wait until you see the crimson sateen dress I've bought for you, and as for the green taffeta . . . '

I broke off, my tea and Gertrude's new dresses quite forgotten as I began to read Aunt Cassie's letter.

'What is it, Miss Selina?' Gertrude's sharpness was gone, and now she was all concern. 'You've gone quite pale. Is something wrong?'

I let the letter drop to my lap, waiting a moment or two before replying.

'Yes . . . yes, I rather think there is.'

'Well? What is it? Is your aunt ill?'

I nodded, feeling moisture behind my eyes. Despite the many miles which had separated us, Cassie and I had grown very close through our correspondence.

'Yes, she's ill. It's her heart, and the doctor says she hasn't long to live.'

Gertrude frowned.

'Well I never. She's not said a word about heart trouble before, has she?'

'Not once. Indeed, judging by what she has told me of her daily routine, one might be forgiven for thinking she had the constitution of a horse.'

'Perhaps it's come on sudden like.'

'No.' I glanced down at the letter. 'She's known about it for some time, but she says she didn't want to worry me, especially when I was so far away. But there's more than that,

5

Gertie. I don't understand the rest of what she says.'

Gertrude was pouring herself a good strong cup of Indian tea from the second pot, for she had no time for what she called scented dill-water.

'Well, I'm not brighter than you, Miss Selina, that's for sure, but maybe if you told me . . .'

'I'll read you what she says. Perhaps I'm being obtuse. Listen to this.'

' 'For fifteen years I have kept to myself something which I should have divulged a long time ago. It has weighed on my soul all these years, but never more than now, when I know that my life is nearing its end. I cannot go to my Maker without telling someone, yet there is no one here in whom I can confide, nor dare I commit it to paper.

'You are my beloved sister's child, and so the blood-tie between us is strong, and I know that you will understand my reasons for keeping silent. So, dearest Selina, only to you can I confess my weakness. Now that you are home again, please come as soon as you can, for time may be shorter than we think.' '

Gertrude and I sat and looked at one another in silence for a whole minute. Then Gertie took another sip and said thoughtfully:

6

'Odd that. Doesn't sound like Miss Van Doren at all, but perhaps it's because she's ill. What can it possibly be that she's kept to herself for so long, and couldn't tell, say, the vicar or her doctor? And hasn't she got a nephew in Leyden too?'

'Yes, my cousin, Anthony Sewall, but you know she doesn't care for him. Her other sister married a man whom Cassie disliked intensely, and I'm afraid that poor Anthony suffers because of it. She can be quite waspish about him, you know, although she's allowed him to use a small cottage some way from the house. He's an artist, I understand, but Aunt Cassie says he will have a job persuading anyone that this is so, seeing he has an eye neither for line nor colour.'

'What about her friends?'

'I don't think she has many. She's mentioned a few from time to time, but I've gained the impression that she has no intimates. Perhaps that's why she will only talk to me.'

'I don't like it.' Gertrude's lips thinned. 'I think it's dangerous.'

'Dangerous! Oh come, why should it be?' I removed my new hat. Somehow the piece of nonsense seemed inappropriate at that moment. 'Whatever Aunt Cassie's dark secret

7

is, it can't be all that dire, or she wouldn't have been able to keep quiet about it for so long.'

'Oh yes she would,' returned Gertrude grimly. 'Remember, I knew your aunt. A woman of steel, she was, when I last saw her, and I doubt that she's changed much. If she had had to keep silent for a hundred years, she'd have done it. She only wants to talk of it now, seeing that she's . . . '

'Dying? Yes, but that still doesn't make whatever it is something sinister.'

'Then why doesn't she write to you about it? She says she dare not commit it to paper. Why not, if it's some minor matter? And why won't she tell someone in Leyden? I'll tell you why. She doesn't trust those around her. Something must have happened fifteen years ago; something in the village maybe. Perhaps she doesn't know how many of the people there were involved, and so she has kept it to herself. She's afraid of someone or something.'

I pursed my lips. Put like that, it did sound rather frightening, but I told myself I was a soldier's daughter, and that this was no time to be nervous. After all, Gertie might be quite wrong. What could possibly have happened in that sleepy village so long ago which would make Gertrude's woman

8

of steel shy away from her duty and cause her fear?

'We shall have to go,' I said finally. 'There's nothing else for it. When you've finished tea, tell the clerk we're leaving in the morning and make arrangements for our travel. I shall send a telegram to say that we are coming on a visit. Aunt Cassie has a companion, an Isa Hedley. Cassie says Isa is a mouse-woman, whatever that may mean, but presumably she will be able to deal with my message, and assure my aunt that I am on my way.'

When Gertie had gone, I looked at the note once more. The thought of Cassie dying was making my heart ache, but the fear and anguish which I could read between the lines troubled me even more. Gertie was right, of course; this wasn't something trivial. I sat back for a moment, trying to make sense of it. A seventy-year-old woman of considerable means, living a sedate and rather dull life in a tucked-away village in the heart of the English countryside, suddenly revealing the existence of a secret which had gnawed at her cruelly for many long years.

Notwithstanding my determination to shew no alarm, I gave a small shudder. Gertie was right about that too; it did sound rather dangerous.

★ ★ ★

In spite of my anxiety to reach Cassie as soon as possible, it took us nearly a week to reach our destination. First, Gertrude had a bad migraine, an affliction to which she was prone, which lasted for two days. Then, some of our luggage was mislaid and another precious day passed before it could be found. At York, there was more confusion about the carriage which was to take us on to Leyden, and a further twenty-four hours spent fuming and fretting whilst this misunderstanding was unravelled.

I had looked at Cassie's letter a dozen times or more during our wait, trying to read something into it which would make sense. I failed miserably, and finally burnt the note in accordance with the instructions in her postscript. Obviously, my aunt did not want anyone to know the real reason for my visit.

Once the letter had gone, I felt lost; it was as if the whole thing had been a figment of my imagination. Only when I spoke of the matter again to Gertrude was I reassured that my mind had not invented it.

As we grew nearer to Leyden we could see the Moors stretching round us on all sides. I was overwhelmed, for I had never seen anything like them before. Green and smooth, rolling off into infinity, touched here and there with purple heather. They were timeless, like something in a dream.

I could have watched them for hours, save for my mounting desire to reach Steeple Court, and then, finally, we were turning in through a pair of wrought iron gates and clipclopping up a path neatly bordered by flowering shrubs and laurel bushes.

Cassie had described her house to me more than once, yet even so I was not prepared for the beauty of the early Georgian structure, with its warm, mellowed bricks set against a high screen of trees. There were well-tended gardens on each side, and beyond the house to the left I could see a little copse.

'Isn't it charming?' I whispered to Gertrude, but before she could answer, the front door was opening to us, and I found myself staring down at a small woman of indeterminate years. Her dull brown hair was drawn up into a tight knot on top of her head, and her drab grey dress innocent of any trimming. I had no need to ask who she was, for I recognised Cassie's mouse-woman at once.

'Miss Hedley?' I smiled, trying to put her at her ease, for she was patently nervous. 'I am Selina Rochford, and my aunt is expecting me.'

Whilst I had not anticipated an effusive welcome from Cassie's paid companion, I was totally unprepared for the effect of my announcement. Isa's long pink nose twitched slightly and then, without warning, she burst into tears.

Fortunately, I was not required to deal with the Mouse's extraordinary behaviour, for a second later a man crossed the hall towards us. He said a few words to Isa Hedley, which I could not catch, reducing her to merciful silence. Then he turned to me with a rueful smile.

'My dear Miss Rochford, I'm so sorry about this. Take no notice of Isa; she's very upset at the moment. My name is Stannard; Dr. David Stannard. Shall we go into the drawing-room?'

I was only too grateful to do so, following him across the hall and leaving Gertrude to deal with the lachrymose Mouse.

I took a quick look round the room. Cassie had resisted the tide of the ornate, over-carved, fussiness of modern furniture, content to retain the marvellous simplicity of an earlier age. I half-expected to see a footman in powdered wig and knee-breeches gliding silently past the Adam fireplace. Then my eye caught the portrait above the mantelpiece, and for a second I forgot Dr.

Stannard's existence. I knew at once that it was Cassie. She was tall for a woman, with a breadth about her shoulders which betokened strength. Her silver-grey hair was piled up at the back of her head, and her dark, painted eyes seemed to be looking directly at me, as if assessing the quality of the niece she had not seen for so long.

Finally I came back to earth, and said apologetically:

'Do forgive me, Dr. Stannard. I haven't seen my aunt since I was two and so, of course, I know nothing of her appearance. Is this a good likeness?'

Stannard nodded. He was about thirty, not over-tall but well-built, with crisp brown hair, neat beard, and a nice smile.

'Yes it is. It was painted some four years ago by a distinguished London artist. Yes, she was very like that.'

The silence lasted for several seconds. Then I said unsteadily:

'Was, Dr. Stannard?'

He made no pretence about it, quite blunt as he gave me the details.

'Yes, I'm afraid so. She died five days ago. She'd been gardening, a thing I had forbidden her to do, but, of course, she took no notice of me. When she got back to the house, she collapsed and never regained consciousness. You can comfort yourself with the fact that she did not suffer.'

'I see.'

I must have sounded rather forlorn, for Stannard said quickly:

'I'm sorry if I broke the news to you too abruptly. I'm afraid my bedside manner leaves a lot to be desired. Can I get you anything? Some brandy?'

'No, no thank you.' I looked back at the portrait. 'I'm quite all right, and after all there really is no way of softening the blow, is there? It's just that I hadn't expected her to go so soon.'

'Neither had I.' Stannard led me to a chair, touching me lightly on the shoulder as if to comfort me. 'I thought she would live a month or two more, but one can never tell in these cases.'

'She asked me to come and visit her. Did you know that?'

'Yes, I knew that she wanted to see you, once you had returned to England, and before she . . . well . . . before she died.'

Stannard seemed such a sympathetic and sensible sort of man that for a moment I was tempted to confide in him about Cassie's last letter. Then I stopped myself. If Cassie had wanted him to know what was in her mind, she would have told him herself. I pushed the thought away and turned to more practical matters.

'When is the funeral?'

'To-morrow. All the arrangements have been made. We knew you were on your way and assumed you would want matters put in hand. Your aunt's solicitor, Cecil Carbury, is already here. The Will is to be read at three o'clock, after the service.'

'Who else is here? In the house, I mean.'

'No one, except Carbury and the staff, so you won't be plagued by anyone. Mrs. Greene was your aunt's housekeeper; a very competent woman. She will see to everything for you. There are two maids, a cook, a scullery wench and, of course the gardener and coachman.'

'And the Mou . . . Miss Hedley.'

Stannard gave a soft laugh.

'The Mouse? Yes, I know what Cassie called her. I fear it was a very apt description, and I doubt if you'll find her much help to you.'

'What about my cousin Anthony?'

Stannard's amusement vanished, and he looked wry.

'Well, as you probably know, Cassie didn't like him. She let him have a run-down old cottage on the edge of the estate, but he very seldom came here to the house.'

15

'Will he be at the funeral?'

'Possibly.'

'And at the reading of the Will?'

Stannard raised his shoulders.

'Again, possibly, if only out of interest, or to meet you. Cassie had made it very clear to him that he could not expect a penny from her, so he may not bother.'

'Who else will be there? I gather Cassie did not have many close friends.'

'No, she didn't. She kept herself to herself, as the villagers say. Indeed, for the last few years she was almost a recluse. However, there will be some present. Colonel Cartwright and his wife; the Fanshawe sisters, who would never miss such an occasion, and Chloe Oldfield.'

'Oldfield? Yes, I believe I remember Cassie mentioning that name. She also spoke of a Marcus Tarrant and a girl called Oriel Stewart. Will they be there?'

Suddenly there was a reserve in Stannard's voice which I did not understand.

'No. Sir Marcus was not a close friend; indeed, he was not a friend at all. And as for Oriel . . . '

'Another of whom Cassie disapproved?'

I tried to speak lightly, to stop the lump forming in my throat. The shock of Stannard's news was now beginning to hit

16

me, and I wanted to bury my face in my hands and cry, just as the Mouse had done.

At first Stannard didn't answer, and when I looked at him his face had grown stern, as if I had said something indecent. Then he sighed.

'No, Miss Rochford, it isn't that. Oriel Stewart is twenty now, but she has the mentality of a child of five. When she was seven, her parents died and Sir Francis Tarrant made her his ward. Now Francis is dead, Marcus, his son, looks after her.'

I felt the colour flood into my cheeks at my appalling gaffe.

'Oh, I'm so sorry. I had no idea . . .'

Stannard thawed at once, his hand on my shoulder again.

'No, of course you hadn't. How could you? You'll like Oriel, despite her sad condition. She's a delightful girl. A pity that Marcus keeps such a tight rein on her; it would do her good to mix more with people.'

I was hardly listening to Stannard, for I was doing some quick mental arithmetic. Oriel was twenty now and had the mentality of a child of five. Did that mean that something had happened when she was five which had stunted her intellectual growth? Something, in fact, which had occurred fifteen years ago?

17

At that moment Mrs. Greene appeared, and Stannard introduced us.

'There, I leave you in good hands, and I shall see you tomorrow. Don't hesitate to call on me if you need anything.'

After he had gone, Mrs. Greene took me upstairs. She was a nice, round little woman, with rosy cheeks and white hair tucked neatly into her starched cap.

When I saw my room I exclaimed with pleasure. It was drenched in sunlight, overlooking the rose-garden, and every piece of the old mahogany furniture had been polished until it looked like glass. The drapes at the windows and round the four-poster were pale green, the Chinese carpet beneath our feet worth a fortune.

'There's a dressing-room off to the right,' said Mrs. Greene, nodding in its direction. 'I've put your maid there for the time being. Later on you may want her to move upstairs with the rest of the servants, but I thought you'd like to have her near to you, seeing this is your first night here.'

'That was very thoughtful of you, Mrs. Greene, but, of course, Gertrude and I may not be staying.'

She turned her head quickly, something like alarm in her eyes.

'Not staying, Miss Selina? Does that mean

18

you would sell Steeple Court?'

'Good heavens, no! But we don't know whether it will belong to me until after the reading of the Will.'

'No worry on that score.' The housekeeper was smiling again, her momentary concern gone. 'Everyone knows Miss Cassie intended you to have the house.'

'But many a slip, you know.'

'Not in this case. After all, she had no one else.'

Mrs. Greene had obviously dismissed Anthony Sewall as finally as Cassie had done. I was beginning to feel quite sorry for my cousin.

'Dinner at eight, if that suits.'

'It will do splendidly.' My smile faded. 'Will you ask Gertrude to come and see me? I must consider what suitable clothes I have with me for to-morrow. You see, when we left London I hadn't thought that . . . '

'Now, now, don't you upset yourself, Miss Selina.' Mrs. Greene's voice was soothing. 'She wouldn't have felt a thing, and she'd had a good life, bless her.'

When she left me I went to the window and stared down at the rose bushes. That Cassie had not suffered at the moment of her death, I was prepared to believe, but whether she had had a good life was something quite different. If Cassie had worried all that time about something as serious as Gertie insisted it was, then it must have been very far from a tranquil existence.

Now Cassie would never be able to tell me about it. I could feel tears on my cheeks, wiping them away quickly because I didn't want Gertie to find such weakness in me.

And I wouldn't be weak. My aunt had wanted to tell me something, but now she was dead. Therefore, dangerous or not, I would find out what it was without her help. It wouldn't be easy, but that didn't matter; Cassie's life couldn't have been easy either. I turned from the window as Gertie came in, all my emotion was gone as I said in my calmest tone of voice:

'Well, Gertie, what am I going to wear to-morrow?'

* * *

When the elaborate funeral service was over and done with, and the guests had done justice to the cold baked meats prepared by Mrs. Bolan, the cook, I went into the library where Cecil Carbury was sitting at the desk, the Will in his hand.

There were only a few of us there. The servants, Isa Hedley, Dr. Stannard, the incumbent of the local church, and myself.

Each of the servants had been remembered. Mrs. Greene had been given a pension for life, the Mouse a slightly less generous allowance for her services. A few hundred pounds had been set aside for the repair of the church roof, and David Stannard was made trustee of a further sum to be used for the relief of poverty in the village.

Then Carbury got down to the serious business. I listened in stunned silence as he read the Will. Not only had Cassie left me Steeple Court; she had also left me the residue of her fortune of forty thousand pounds.

Whilst I was still reeling from such generosity, Carbury said irritably:

'Your aunt also left you all her jewellery, Miss Rochford, but there is a problem.'

'Oh? What kind of problem?'

The solicitor frowned, obviously put out.

'We cannot find any jewellery. Naturally, I assumed it was in Miss Van Doren's bank, but it's not. Mrs. Greene and I have had a good look here; we thought you would not object.'

'No, of course not.' I pulled myself together. 'Perhaps she sold it. How long ago was the Will drawn up?'

'It was revised only last year, and I am

certain she did not sell it. She refers to the jewellery as of immense value. Had she sold any of it, presumably her bankers would have received the proceeds in due course.'

'Could it have been stolen?'

Carbury gave a short laugh.

'No, indeed not. Your aunt was a generous woman, but if anyone had tried to cheat her, including stealing from her, she would have been quick to let everyone know about it. No, the jewels must be here in the house somewhere. Perhaps you will have another search made.'

'Of course. And that is all my aunt says in her Will?'

'No, there's one more thing. I'll read the clause.'

Knowing how obscure and lengthy such legal documents could be, I said hastily:

'That is not necessary, Mr. Carbury. Just tell me in simple terms what it is.'

Carbury grunted and looked at me over the top of his spectacles.

'Very well, it is this. Your aunt asks that you, her heiress, should care for her children who live upstairs. She says she would like you to cherish them as she did during her lifetime.'

I think my mouth must have dropped open

in sheer astonishment, for the solicitor said hastily:

'A figure of speech only, you understand. They are not really children.'

'Then who are they? What on earth did my aunt mean?'

'Did she never write and tell you about her hobby?' Carbury was gazing at me pensively. 'I'm surprised she didn't, for it meant a great deal to her.'

I stole a glance at Stannard's face, but it was impassive. He hadn't mentioned such an all-consuming interest to me, but then our talk had been brief and doubtless he assumed I already knew about it. Then I looked back at the solicitor.

'No, my aunt mentioned nothing like that in any of her letters.' I was beginning to feel uneasy, not at all sure that I liked the sound of Cassie's hobby. 'But if they're not real children, who are they?'

'Not who, Miss Rochford.' For the first time there was a glimmer of humour in Carbury's frosty eyes. 'What, would be a more appropriate word to use. You see, they're not human beings; they are waxworks.'

2

On the following morning, Gertrude and I looked over most of the house, escorted by Mrs. Greene. It was like moving backwards into a different era, and only the spotless kitchen shewed any signs of the current love of knick-knacks in the shape of fairings which the servants had arranged proudly along the mantelshelf and dresser.

Mrs. Bolan was a gaunt woman, immaculate in her voluminous apron, and very civil as she bobbed a welcome. The two parlour-maids, Jessie Trent and Nell Foster, seemed amiable enough, and I had no doubt at all that Mrs. Greene had the pair of them well under control. The scullery maid, Dorcas Lyle, was only fourteen, with large mournful eyes and appeared to have been crying.

'Wants knocking into shape,' said Mrs. Greene of Dorcas as we went upstairs again, 'but she'll do in time. We have two girls come up from the village each day to help with the cleaning, so we manage very well.'

I had luncheon in the large, airy dining-room, eating a light but well-cooked meal from priceless china plates, using a glass of finest-cut crystal. I was finishing my coffee when Jessie Trent appeared.

'Yes, Jessie?'

'Beg pardon, but Miss Hedley says do you want to see the waxworks this afternoon? Room's always kept locked, you see, and she's got the keys.'

So intrigued had I been with the rest of Steeple Court and its lovely gardens, that after my initial misgivings concerning my aunt's rather odd pastime, I had forgotten all about the waxworks, It did seem rather strange that Cassie had never mentioned them to me if they had meant so much to her.

'Yes, I suppose so.' I put my cup down. 'But why is the room kept locked?'

'Was mistress's orders.' Jessie sniffed in chagrin. 'Thought one of us might damage them heathen things, so no one was allowed up there, 'cept Miss Hedley.'

'Then please ask Miss Hedley to come and fetch me in ten minutes, and tell Mrs. Bolan her luncheon was excellent.'

Less than ten minutes later the Mouse appeared, a look of suppressed excitement on her face.

'Am I too early?' She tip-toed over to the table as if she thought I might snap at her for her promptness. I can easily come back if . . . '

'No, no.' I rose at once, smiling encouragingly. 'I'm quite ready, and looking forward to seeing the waxworks.'

I was not at all sure that that was a true statement, for I still felt that same unease as when Mr. Carbury had first informed me of their existence, but I followed Isa dutifully to the top of the house and watched her insert the key almost reverently into the lock.

I don't really know what I had expected. At most, I suppose, a small room with a few amateurish models, poked inside out of everybody's way. I couldn't have been more wrong.

It wasn't a room at all, but a wide gallery which must have run the full width of the house on the east side. In order to shew off the figures, Aunt Cassie had had the walls papered dark grey, with curtains and carpet to match.

And there they were, Cassie's 'children': so life-like that for a second I expected some of them to come forward to greet me. On a dais at one end, Cassie had placed her kings and queens: Henry VIII, Anne Boleyn, Elizabeth, Henry V, Mary Queen of Scots, and the ill-fated Marie-Antoinette.

I walked over to them, conscious that Isa

was following me closely. I stared at them, marvelling at the skill which had produced the perfect flesh-tones of their faces, the glass eyes which looked so real, and the patience and love which had gone into the fashioning of their richly ornate costumes.

But there was more than a handful of royalty to bemuse one. Cassie had prepared a few tableaux through the centre of the gallery: a gipsy encampment; a cell in Newgate Prison, with four felons crouched on dirty straw; a group of elderly ladies in dark silk dresses and crisp lace collars, seated round a table as if they were engaged in earnest conversation.

Finally I turned to the Mouse, who was watching me in high delight.

'I can't believe it,' I said almost breathlessly. 'I had not expected anything like this. They look so real. That gipsy boy, for instance; it is as though he is about to speak.'

Isa giggled.

'Yes, he's new. The last one Miss Cassie dressed before she died.'

'But who made them? The figures, I mean.'

'There was a man called Porter who had a travelling waxworks show. He came this way a long time ago, and when Miss Van Doren saw his models, there was nothing for

27

it but that she must have her own collection. He came twice a year after that, and made one or two figures each time, in accordance with your aunt's instructions. She gave him exact details, and made the most meticulous drawings for him to follow.'

'How long ago was that? When my aunt first met Mr. Porter.'

Isa's brow puckered.

'I suppose it must be some fifteen years now.'

Again I felt the twinge of something near to fear. That ominous figure once more, but it could only be coincidence. Cassie's meeting with Mr. Porter couldn't possibly have had anything to do with her secret, nor could her rather bizarre hobby.

'How many are there?' I turned my head, seeing more clusters of figures at the far end of the gallery. 'There seem to be dozens.'

'There are thirty.' The Mouse was in her element, and clearly she cared as much about the collection as Cassie had done. 'I was allowed to help, you know. Miss Van Doren let me sew some of the costumes and make the jewellery.'

'Mr. Porter must have been very clever.' I was looking at the gipsy boy again. It was rather terrifying to be so close to something I knew to be lifeless, yet which must surely move at any moment. 'How was it done?'

The Mouse was only too anxious to tell me.

'Well, he used to make a clay model of the head from your aunt's sketches and notes. When that was dry, he covered it with plaster of Paris, made in sections, fitted with sockets, so that the pieces could be removed easily and later joined together again. When the plaster was ready, he would take it off bit by bit and then reassemble it, tying the parts carefully together.'

Isa glanced at me quickly.

'This does not bore you, Miss Rochford?'

'No indeed not. Please go on.'

'After that, Mr. Porter would pour the hot wax through the hole at the bottom of the cast. The wax cooled from the outside, you see, and when it had set to a thickness of about one and a half inches, the surplus wax was poured off. As soon as the hollow mask was really set, Mr. Porter would remove the pieces of plaster again. Of course there were tiny lines left where the plaster had been joined, and he had to scrape these away very carefully. It was a most delicate job.'

'It must have been. But the colouring; it's so natural. How was that done?'

Isa looked mildly put out.

'We never knew. It was his secret and it

29

died with him. He met with an accident last year. Such a loss. Your aunt was desolate, for she had many more sketches ready for him. Mr. Porter used to boast that his faces were every bit as good as those made by Marie Grosholtz.'

'Marie who?'

Isa preened herself, smug with superior knowledge.

'Perhaps you know her better by her married name. It was Tussaud. She's dead too, of course, but they say the exhibition which her family still carries on in the Portman Rooms at Baker Street in London is a marvel to behold.'

The Mouse gave me a key, smiling hopefully.

'Would you like me to go on looking after them for you?'

'Oh please.' Suddenly I wanted to get out of the gallery, feeling hemmed in by something I couldn't explain. 'I should be afraid of damaging them.'

'Here's the workroom.' Isa was determined that I should miss nothing, and led me to one end of the hall where a large room, with a door leading to the back stairs, had been shelved to accommodate the bales of silver tissue, satin, silk, velvet, and brocade, as well as the plaster casts which, it seemed, were never thrown away. There were boxes of paste jewellery, wigs, shoes and fans, as well as plainer materials for the poorer of my aunt's children.

As we left the gallery I said slowly:

'What did my aunt's friends make of the collection?'

Isa sniffed contemptuously.

'They only saw it once or twice, and then they weren't interested.'

'Not even my cousin? I should have thought that as he is an artist, he would have appreciated it.'

I turned as I spoke, just in time to see the besotted look on Isa Hedley's face, her voice softening as she answered.

'Oh yes, he is an artist, but he only saw the figures once.' Her brows met in a frown. 'He wasn't welcome here, you know, although why your aunt could not see his worth, I'm sure I don't know. He is so handsome and talented that . . . '

She broke off in embarrassment, probably noticing my expression of surprise. It was clear that whatever Cassie had thought of Anthony Sewall, the Mouse was wholly under his spell.

'Did he like them?'

Isa was honest, despite her obvious infatuation for my cousin.

31

'I don't think he did really. He said they were artificial.'

'Perhaps he was right, yet that gipsy boy . . . '

'Well, of course, he didn't see that one. As I told you, that was the last one we did. Mr. Sewall hasn't been up here for five years or more.'

By this time we had reached the hall, and Isa made her excuses and scurried away. Cassie had been right; she really was just like a little mouse. I stood for a moment looking up through the well of the staircase. The wax figures were splendid, of course; works of art in their own way. Yet the uncomfortable feeling that I had had since I first heard about them was growing stronger. It was as if part of my house had been taken over by an army of strangers.

I told myself I was a fool, and went in search of Gertrude.

★ ★ ★

One week later I held my first At Home. I soon learnt from Mrs. Greene that it was the custom in Leyden for such hospitality to be offered at frequent intervals, and it seemed to me as good a way as any to get to know some of my neighbours.

Furthermore, it would enable me to take the bull by the horns and ask my guests whether they had any recollection of some unusual happening in the village at the period in question, as otherwise I should stand no chance of finding out what had been worrying Cassie so.

The first to arrive were David Stannard and Chloe Oldfield. I was glad to see Stannard once more, for I thought him a pleasant young man, and I had taken a liking to Chloe from the moment I met her after the funeral. She was a small woman, probably in her late twenties, but her heart-shaped face, violet eyes, and enchanting smile made her seem younger. Her hair was copper-coloured, and she had dared to wear a pink outfit which ought to have been a catastrophe, but was, in fact, quite the opposite.

'I'm so glad to see you again,' she said, and I knew she was taking in every detail of my face and pale blue gown. 'We couldn't talk properly last time we met. I was told that you were as beautiful as your mother, Margaret, but it isn't true. You're far lovelier than the portrait of her in the library.'

I was a trifle taken aback by Chloe's outspokenness, but she soon laughed my awkwardness away.

'Take no notice of my wayward tongue,

Selina. David will tell you that I'm seldom conventional, and often tactless, but I really mean well, don't I?'

'Not always.' Stannard gave me a wink. 'She's a minx: don't let her tell you otherwise.'

'Don't be horrid, David.' She pulled a face at him. 'You'll give Selina the wrong idea about me. Oh Lord, here's Colonel Cartwright and his awful wife. How can she wear such a dreadful shade of purple, and I swear that that frock is ten years old, if it's a day.'

'You're a bitch, Chloe,' said Stannard calmly. 'As a penance, go and tell her how well she looks, and bring her over to see Selina.'

'We are very informal here.' Stannard was amused at the look on my face. 'We use each other's Christian names, and never hesitate to call a spade a spade. Will you mind that, do you think?'

I relaxed and gave a small laugh.

'No, I don't think I will. In fact, it will be something of a relief. For some reason, my aunt's letters to me led me to suppose that people here were rather . . .'

'Stuffy?' He joined in my laugh. 'Some are, of course, but not all of us.'

When I had greeted the colonel and his

34

wife, and the two Misses Fanshawe, Ursula and Jane, Mr. Blake the incumbent of St. Martin's arrived, and asked anxiously after my health and spiritual well-being. Having assured him that both were in good order, I rang for tea. I had invited Sir Marcus Tarrant and his ward, but had received his cool and somewhat bleak refusal for them both. I had also invited my cousin, but since he was just as likely to refuse as Tarrant, I saw no reason to wait for him.

Tea was served in the drawing-room, Gertrude helping Jessie because Nell Foster had the toothache and wouldn't stop crying. I was in charge of the tea-pot and great silver kettle on the spirit stove, whilst Gertie and Jessie moved amongst the guests with wafer-thin sandwiches and an array of iced cakes and biscuits sufficient to feed an army.

'How I hate you for having Mrs. Bolan.' Chloe was sitting next to me, sampling a cucumber sandwich. 'If I ever get the chance to steal her from you I shall, so be warned.'

'She wouldn't leave Steeple Court,' said David idly, 'so you need have no fear, Selina. Well, well.' His tone changed and he sat upright in his chair. 'We are indeed honoured. Here is Anthony.'

'Oh good!' Chloe gave a malicious chuckle.

'Now we shall have some fun, for he's more outrageous than I am; just wait and see.'

I rose to greet my cousin with some trepidation. I had imagined him to be a thin, willowy young man, with a lock of hair falling negligently over his brow, and long delicate fingers capable of wielding the finest of paintbrushes.

Anthony Sewall was tall, broad of shoulder, and very good-looking. I could see now why the Mouse had fallen in love with him, for his regular features and dark blue eyes were more than enough to make the most hardened of women quiver with emotion.

He ignored my outstretched hand and put his arms round me, giving me a kiss full on the mouth.

'Hallo, my lovely coz. Have you forgiven me for not coming to Cassie's funeral?' He put his head on one side, watching my reaction. 'I thought she'd rather be buried in peace, than turn in her grave at the idea of me standing there laughing at her interment.'

'I told you so.' Chloe held up her face to be kissed as Anthony released me. 'He's far worse than I am, don't you think?'

'When I got my breath back I said quietly:

'I wish you had been there, Anthony, but I understood why you weren't. And I'm sorry about the Will. It was terribly unfair.'

'Not in the least.' Sewall was neither angry nor embittered. 'The old girl told me plainly enough that I wouldn't get a sou from her, and I didn't expect one.'

'I'm told you live in a rather dilapidated cottage.'

'It's not a palace, but it does for my needs.'

'We must change that. There must be somewhere else you can live.'

'Of course.' Chloe clapped her hands. 'What about Dower Cottage? That's a lovely place, although it's not large. So much better than your rat-infested hovel.'

Anthony turned to look at her, his smile fading.

'Chloe, keep your generosity for the distribution of your own belongings. Perhaps Selina has another use for Dower Cottage.'

'Oh but I haven't,' I said hastily, before Chloe's scowl could become a problem. 'I don't even know where it is, but if it is empty, please use it, Anthony. It would make me much happier if you did.'

The bright eyes turned to me again.

'You're thoughtful as well as beautiful, coz. Will you sit for me one day?'

'Well, I . . . '

'Too soon to ask, eh?' He patted my cheek

as if he had known me all my life. 'All right, I'll ask you again later. Meanwhile, my thanks for Dower Cottage. It will be a change to have a roof over my head which doesn't leak.'

'Oh do look!' Chloe was laughing again. 'Aren't they the limit?'

'Who?'

I looked vaguely about me.

'Why the Misses Fanshawe, of course. See, over there. They always sit together and nibble their food like rabbits, and the amount they can get through is quite unbelievable.'

'Chloe!' Stannard wasn't smiling now. 'I don't think they get enough to eat at home. You know damned well how hard up they are.'

'Then they should be honest about it.' She was unmoved by his reprimand. 'They spend all their money, such as it is, on clothes, so that no one shall know that they're poor, and practically starve themselves between one free meal and the next.'

'Chloe!'

'Oh all right!' She turned to me and said softly: 'I'm not really as dreadful as I sound. I'm truly sorry for them, but I wish they went about in rags and filled their stomachs instead. I hate pretence.'

The conversation became general, and I

38

went to talk to my other guests. The Misses Fanshawe did look thin under their neat but inexpensive black gowns and jackets, cheekbones sharp beneath the skin, a fact which I had not noticed when I met them after the funeral. Feeling sick with shame that I had so much, I quickly handed them a plate of Mrs. Bolan's richest chocolate cake, and moved on to the colonel.

After fresh tea had been poured, and there was a slight lull in the conversation, I took my chance. I was not anxious to let any part of Cassie's secret slip from me, nor to tell anyone of the letter I had received when I was in London. Instead, I invented a small lie to see what my guests had to say.

'Do you know,' I said, embracing them all with a smile, 'somehow this makes me think of a note I got from Aunt Cassie once. Why, it must have been fifteen years ago, at least, for I was only a child. She wrote of something very frightening which had happened here in Leyden. I asked her in my reply to tell me more about it, but perhaps by then she had realised I was too young to know the details, and she never mentioned it again. Sitting here with you all in such a peaceful place as this, I just cannot imagine what it could have been, can you?'

I knew every eye was on me: even the

Misses Fanshawe had stopped eating to listen, but it was David who spoke first.

'Something frightening? What sort of something?'

'I've no idea. That's all my aunt said.'

'Fifteen years ago.' Anthony shook his head. 'I can't recall anything startling happening then, can you, Chloe?'

'No, darling, but I was only eleven and you were thirteen. Children never notice what is going on round them, do they? They are far too busy inventing their own mischief.'

'Colonel?' I battled on. 'Does anything occur to you?'

'Can't say it does, m'dear,' he said after a moment's thought. 'It's a long time ago, of course.'

'I've got an excellent memory.' His wife thrust herself quickly into the conversation. She was a thin woman with sandy hair, and Chloe had been quite right about that shade of purple. 'I'd have remembered if anything untoward had gone on. Your aunt must have been mistaken, or you did not understand what she meant.'

'How disappointing.' Chloe wiped her lips with a linen napkin and sighed. 'It would have rounded off the afternoon so nicely if Mrs. Cartwright had remembered something really thrilling, like an axe-murder.'

Anthony laughed, but I thought I heard a harsh note in his voice.

'Don't be a fool, Chloe. People don't murder one another with axes in Leyden. It just isn't done.'

'Misses Fanshawe?'

I plodded on doggedly, watching their rather scared faces as they raised them to mine.

'No, my dear, we don't remember anything out of the way, do we?'

'No, indeed.' Jane was a mere echo of Ursula. 'Nothing at all.'

'Well then, I shall just have to keep asking others, shan't I?' I dismissed the subject as I held out my hand. 'More tea, Anthony?'

When the guests had all gone and Gertrude and I were alone, I said thoughtfully:

'Do you think they were telling the truth?'

'Seemed to be. Like Miss Chloe says, half of them were only children then. They wouldn't remember much. Can't see why the others should lie either. Not that kind, are they?'

'No, they're not, yet you must have been right in your first supposition, Gertie. Something did happen here; something which Cassie was too scared to talk about, and I suspect she was a woman not easily frightened.'

'That's true.'

'Then I must go on asking questions. Perhaps Sir Marcus may be a more fruitful source of information.'

'He'd only have been a lad as well. Don't expect too much from him.'

'I won't, but nor will I give in. Before I'm done, I'll find out what it was.'

'Take care.' Gertie's face had grown paler. 'I don't like this at all, Miss Selina. I told you I thought it was risky.'

'So be it,' I said with more courage than I felt. 'Risky or not, I'm going to find the answer. I owe Aunt Cassie that much, at least.'

★ ★ ★

The next morning I went for a walk round the gardens, amazed at the size of them. In addition to the formal gardens and the copse, there was a stream, an orchard, and a vast kitchen garden from which Mrs. Bolan culled her fresh vegetables and herbs.

When I reached the fence which separated the property from open fields, I saw the gipsy encampment. There were about a dozen men and women in all, together with seven ragged and noisy children. There were three covered waggons and a number of horses grazing on the sweet meadow grass.

Two of the women sat cross-legged by a cauldron, one stirring something with a heavy iron spoon, and then I realised where Aunt Cassie had got her idea for the tableau in the gallery. She must have come and watched the gipsies, just as I was doing now, making notes of their appearances and returning to the house to produce the detailed drawings for the late Mr. Porter.

I turned away quickly, for I didn't want them to see me, but when I reached the house I encountered Isa Hedley.

'I've just seen some gipsies. They look exactly like the figures upstairs.'

The Mouse gave a prim smile.

'Yes, it's hard to tell which are the real ones, isn't it?'

'Are they always there?'

'Oh no. They come once a year, about this time. They stay for a week or two, then they move on.'

'How long have they been coming here?'

I knew what the Mouse was going to say even before she opened her mouth, the sinking feeling in the pit of my stomach growing stronger.

'For about fifteen years or so, I think. They're not just ordinary gipsies, you know. They're true Romanies.'

She went on her way. I wasn't sure what difference there was between an ordinary gipsy and a true Romany, but of one thing I was certain. That inevitable figure had cropped up yet again. I turned to look back in the direction of the meadows. Could Cassie have had anything to do with the Romanies, apart from sketching them for her wax figures? Was it something to do with them which had frightened her, and become a burden on her soul? It was a possibility, and I decided that in a day or two I would steel myself and go and talk to them.

If no one in Cassie's social circle could help me, perhaps the Romanies could. It was worth a try at any rate.

★ ★ ★

I was surprised to find how easily I slipped into the routine of Steeple Court and of the village of Leyden generally. Within two weeks I had dined with Colonel and Mrs. Cartwright, taken tea with the Misses Fanshawe in their shabby but spotlessly clean parlour, and become firm friends with Chloe Oldfield, whom I saw almost every day. I had visited my cousin, who had moved into Dower Cottage, still evading his request that

44

I should sit for him, but liking him more each time I saw him.

I had even grown used to the Mouse, who spent most of her time with the waxworks. I still had to force myself to enter the gallery, usually choosing a time when Isa was not there. I felt I must get used to them by myself, and learn not to tremble slightly as I walked amongst them. I made a point of going to look at them at least once a day, hoping that familiarity would breed contempt, but it didn't. I found that I could contemplate Henry VIII and Elizabeth the Virgin Queen, without a qualm, for I knew them to be long-dead. The quiver only started when I looked at the old ladies sitting at the table, for two of them were so like Ursula and Jane Fanshawe that I half-expected them to look round and smile at me as I passed by. Worst of all was the gipsy boy, and I had to use every ounce of my self-control to stand in front of him and meet the dark eyes fringed with lashes as natural as my own. It really was an incredible piece of work, and I never once dared to glance over my shoulder after I had left him, in case he had turned to watch me go.

The house ran smoothly in Mrs. Greene's capable hands and, fortunately, she and Gertrude got on well together. Gertrude acted as my personal maid, whilst Mrs. Greene was the housekeeper and so, each respecting the other's position, they kept the harmony of the daily routine without difficulty.

One day, however, Mrs. Green came to report that Dorcas Lyle was leaving. Her parents had found her another position in a village two miles away. The exact reason for her departure was not clear either to Mrs. Greene or myself, and the housekeeper was vexed that she had wasted so much time on training the girl.

It was very fortunate, therefore, that before Mrs. Greene had to search for a replacement, Chloe arrived to take tea with me and to beg a favour.

'Dearest Selina, as Steeple Court is so large and must need many hands to keep it in such apple-pie order, do you think you could find a place for another scullery maid?'

I looked at her in surprise.

'Scullery maid? Why, does yours want to desert you as mine has deserted me?'

'You mean Dorcas is going?'

'I'm afraid so. Mrs. Greene is very cross about it too.'

'But what a marvellous piece of luck!' Chloe wore lime-green satin that day, swathed over her hips and floating down to a graceful train which she managed with great skill. 'No, it's not my girl, but a child called Bethia Tudball. Her parents have just died of fever, and I promised to try to find a position for her. She's nearly fourteen, and whilst I don't think she's very intelligent, she is strong and seems willing enough. Will you take her?'

'If Mrs Greene agrees, I should be delighted to do so.'

'What a relief!' Chloe sank back in her chair with a sigh. 'I realised afterwards how rash I had been to offer to find Bethia a job, for it might have taken me weeks.'

Later, Mrs. Greene was called upon to see Bethia, a rather squat girl with a narrow forehead and what I thought were somewhat sly eyes, and pronounced her suitable. Chloe kissed my cheek in thankfulness that her duty had been so easily performed, and Bethia went off to the kitchens with Jessie Trent and Nell Foster.

I thought no more about her until strange rumours began to reach me via Gertie.

'You cannot be serious,' I said, as Gertrude brushed my hair with slow, even strokes. 'Are you really telling me that a heavy saucepan flew across the kitchen?'

'Well, I didn't see it myself.' Gertie's lips were compressed. 'But Jessie and Nell did, and it took Mrs. Greene and me a full ten minutes to stop Nell's hysterics. And that's not all.'

'Good heavens, what else?'

I stared at Gertrude in the dressing-table mirror.

'Well, there was the matter of the cups and saucers.'

'Did they fly across the room too?'

'No, they rattled as if someone were shaking them, and then they fell to the ground in smithereens, but there was no one near them.'

I turned to look at Gertrude, seeing the pallor of her face. Apparently even she had not been immune to the weird goings-on below stairs.

'But, if no one was near them, how could they . . . ?'

'We don't know, but I saw the cellar door open and shut by itself half a dozen times or more, making enough noise to wake the dead.'

'I don't understand this at all. If there is no one there, how can these things happen? What does Mrs. Greene say?'

'She thinks it's a poltergeist, Miss Selina.'

'Oh, Gertie!'

'You can laugh if you will, but what else can it be? Mrs. G. says there's never been

48

nothing like this at Steeple Court before.'

'I should hope not. Is Mrs. Greene nervous?'

'Well, she don't like it no more than I do, but she's a sensible woman. She says to wait a bit and see what else happens. If it goes on, she thinks we ought to speak to the vicar about it.'

'Yes, perhaps we had.' I turned back to the mirror, frowning slightly. 'But there may be some perfectly ordinary explanation for it, you know. Perhaps the wind . . .'

'No, it were calm enough, and don't forget it's happened more than once.'

We said no more that night, but two days later Nell was screaming again, because two heavy storage jars had, to use her own words, jumped across the larder like mad devils.

When I told Chloe of the incidents, she roared with laughter.

'Oh, Selina, what fun! You've got a ghost.'

'A poltergeist, Mrs. Greene says.'

'Almost the same thing, isn't it? What are you going to do?'

'I don't really know. Nothing for the moment.'

'And how is my Bethia getting on? Is she scared by your demons?'

'I have no idea.' I was annoyed with Chloe for making a joke of the affair, for whatever the cause of the disturbances, they were most upsetting and frightening for my staff. 'I suppose she's nervous too.'

'I doubt it.' Chloe must have seen my slight irritation for she became serious at once. 'She's a stolid child with no imagination. Don't worry about it, love, it will pass off. Tell me, have you seen Marcus Tarrant yet?'

'No, nor his ward. Since he refused my first invitation so emphatically, I have not sent him any further notes.' My anger was diverted from Chloe to the unfriendly master of The Grange. 'I don't think I like the sound of him at all.'

Chloe was smiling, but in quite a different way.

'He's very handsome.'

There was something in her voice which made me look at her more closely. Her eyes had a dreamy look about them, half-closed as if she had forgotten that I was there.

'Oh? What sort of person is he? Do you know him well?'

'Well enough. As to what kind of man he is . . . ' The smile deepened. 'The best-looking I have ever seen, although he can be cold and hard, especially when he is angry.'

I said nothing, waiting for Chloe to go on.

'He is foolishly indulgent with Oriel, and far too protective.' Her small rouged mouth was suddenly tight. 'He should never have taken on such a burden.'

'Perhaps he had no choice,' I said mildly. 'If the poor girl was his father's ward . . . '

'She should be put away somewhere, then Marcus might have time for . . . '

We sat silently for a second or two. Then Chloe pulled a face.

'Well, you might as well know the truth; you'll hear it soon enough anyway. I love him. If I hadn't told you, Anthony or David would have done so eventually. They think I'm a fool, but I can't help it.'

'And does he return your feelings?'

'Not noticeably.' She was wry, mocking herself. 'Sometimes he is hardly aware of me, but then . . . just now and then . . . he seems to see me properly. Once, I thought he was going to kiss me, but Oriel came into the room and he moved away from me as if I were poison-ivy.'

'Oh dear.'

She managed another smile, but I felt it was an effort for her.

'Don't be sorry for me, Selina; you'll make me cry. I'm used to Marcus and his ways, and one day perhaps . . . '

'I hope so.' I was not sure what to say.

Flippant though Chloe was on so many occasions, it was obvious that her feelings for Tarrant were deep and true. 'As you say, perhaps one day . . . '

After a while she bade me good-bye and went on her way, reminding me that we were dining with David Stannard on the following evening. I was about to go to my room when Gertrude appeared, and even from a distance I could see that she was shaking.

'Gertie! What is it? What's happened?'

'The bells, Miss Selina. It's the bells this time.'

'The bells? What on earth are you talking about? What bells?'

'The bells in the kitchen. They've all been ringing at once, as if someone was pulling the cords in every blessed room in the house.'

'But . . . '

'But no one rang them.' Gertrude shivered, despite the heat of the day. 'They rang by themselves. Oh, Miss Selina, whatever are we going to do?'

3

After the mysterious ringing of the bells there followed two days of peace, with no further signs of malignant manifestations in the servants' quarters. I sighed with relief, dismissing the matter as one of those quirkish twists of fate which can never properly be explained.

On the third day, I went for a stroll in the fields beyond the copse, well away from the gipsies. I had not been walking for long before I saw someone not far ahead of me. It was a girl, and she was dancing with a curiously wild, yet graceful, abandonment, her pale gold hair loose about her shoulders or swirling out like a fan as she spun round. She wore a white dress with a full skirt, not at all in fashion, and as I drew closer I saw that she had taken off her shoes and stockings. She stopped when she saw me, and I thought for one moment that she was going to run away, but she didn't. She stood motionless until I had covered the last few yards between us.

She was truly beautiful, with the finest of complexions, the high cheekbones lightly touched with a natural hint of pink. Her mouth was ruby red, her huge blue eyes as clear and innocent as a child's.

'Hallo, Oriel,' I said softly, smiling so that she would realise I meant her no harm. 'I am Selina.'

'Selina.'

She repeated it carefully, as if she were learning a lesson, still considering me cautiously.

'I live at Steeple Court. Do you know where that is?'

She nodded and pointed behind me.

'That's right, and you live at The Grange, don't you?'

'Yes, with Marcus.' Quite unexpectedly Oriel smiled, and it lit up her face in a way which made me catch my breath. 'I love Marcus.'

I paused to consider, somewhat sourly, that Marcus Tarrant appeared to have an uncanny knack of making beautiful women fall in love with him, but then I checked myself. Oriel would not understand what being in love meant. Her feelings for Tarrant were of a wholly different order from Chloe's.

'You dance very well,' I said finally, not quite sure what to say to a girl whose body was seductively mature in the curve of its hips and the gentle swell of the breasts, but whose mind had remained frozen since early childhood. 'Do you often come here?'

'Sometimes.' Oriel did another pirouette. 'Now and then I go into the woods. Can you dance?'

I reflected on the somewhat stilted waltzes and polkas which I had trodden with my father's fellow-officers, and laughed inwardly.

'Yes, but not as well as you do.'

We watched one another in silence, while I braced myself to question Oriel before she darted away, for she seemed poised for flight like a wild creature trapped by something it didn't understand. It was difficult to accept the fact that she thought as a child, but I tried to frame my words so that she would understand me.

'Did you know my aunt, Miss Van Doren?'

Oriel nodded vigorously.

'Yes, she didn't like me. Whenever she saw me, she ran away.'

For a moment I was taken aback. I could not imagine a seventy-year-old woman rushing from someone as harmless as Oriel Stewart, least of all Aunt Cassie, and I said quickly:

'Oh, I'm sure she didn't dislike you. Why should she?'

'I don't know.' The azure eyes were solemn and rather sad. 'But she did, I know she did.

I used to go to see the gipsies. She was there many times, watching them too, but she always went away when she saw me.'

I gave up and tried a different approach.

'I can't dance as well as you, but I am very good at remembering things. I can recall incidents which happened ages ago.'

'So can I!' Oriel's swift response was the boasting of a child. 'I expect I'm better at it than you.'

'I doubt it. Why, I can remember a doll I had when I was ten.' I was very casual. 'She had a yellow frock and a frilled petticoat. Can you remember having a doll?'

'I've got dolls now.' Oriel clasped her hands together as if the thought of them brought her pleasure. 'I've got at least twenty, and Marcus bought me a new one last week when he went to York.'

I paused again to consider Marcus Tarrant in the role of guardian to this strange girl, entering a toy shop and purchasing a doll. I found that it taxed my imagination a little too far, and so I continued with my queries.

'If you can remember things so well, can you think back and tell me what happened here in the village about fifteen years ago?'

The smile was gone now, and the eyes fixed on mine looked almost sightless. I felt a brute, but I had to go on.

'Something very frightening happened here then, didn't it, Oriel? Something terrible. You know what it was, don't you? Tell me about it.'

She whimpered, and I watched her mouth droop, tears flooding her eyes. When she began to sob, I was stricken with remorse, helpless as she shook with the intensity of her grief.

I was on the point of moving forward to try to undo the damage I had caused when I heard the sound of horse's hooves thudding over the grass, and in another second the rider was upon us.

I knew at once who it was, and felt violent shock mingle with my guilt as I stared up at Marcus Tarrant's angry face. Chloe had been quite right. He was remarkably handsome, with blond hair, eyes tawny in hue, and features almost without a flaw. Now, in his fury, his face looked like something carved in stone, and the line of his mouth made me step back hastily.

'In God's name what have you done to her?' His voice was as icy as his face, and for a moment I thought he was going to strike me with his riding crop. 'How dare you do this?'

My mouth was dry and my legs none too

steady, but I wasn't going to let Tarrant get away with that, and I said coldly:

'I have done nothing to her. We were merely talking and suddenly Oriel started to cry.'

'Don't lie to me.' The words bit harder than any whip would have done. 'She doesn't cry without reason. What did you say to her, damn you?'

I ground my teeth at his tone.

'I asked her if she knew what happened here in Leyden many years ago.' I was growing angry myself now. 'Does that sound like a criminal offence to you, Sir Marcus?'

'She can't remember anything. Surely that is obvious, even to you.'

'She remembered my aunt.'

He bared his teeth.

'So do I, but you know what I meant. Oriel has no memory of things long past. What sort of woman are you, Miss Rochford, who would torment a child in this way?'

'She is not a child,' I returned steadily. 'She is twenty years old, and I had a very good reason for asking what I did. I had no idea that it would upset her so, but my question was not a frivolous one.'

We glared at each other in hostility, almost forgetting Oriel, whose cries had now subsided.

'I don't care what your reasons were,' said Tarrant finally, 'nor how good you consider them to be. Don't ever question my ward again, or I will see to it that you regret it.'

I opened my mouth to offer a suitable retort, but Marcus had urged his horse forward, leaning from the saddle to catch Oriel round the waist, pulling her up with one arm.

I marvelled at his strength, for Oriel was no featherweight, but when I saw his hand on her body, and her lips touch his cheek, a completely new and totally unexpected emotion went through me, as if I had been jabbed with a knife.

'Remember, Miss Rochford.' Tarrant turned his mount's head, looking down at me again as if he would have liked to crush me under its hooves. 'Leave my ward alone, or you will answer to me for it.'

I watched them race off, my cheeks stinging with unwonted colour. If I had known him, he had certainly been in no doubt as to my identity either. I wondered how he had been so sure who I was, since we had never met, but I pushed the thought aside as I made for home.

I couldn't imagine what had made Chloe Oldfield fall in love with him, for he was more insulting than any man I had ever met before. He was also more violent than any I had encountered, and I had no doubt at all that the threats he had uttered were far from idle.

As I reached the house, I paused. However unpleasant my first meeting with Marcus Tarrant had been, one thing was certain. Oriel Stewart, mentally retarded or not, had understood me. If she did not know what I meant when I asked her about the past, why had she cried so bitterly? I compressed my lips. Threats or no threats from Tarrant, I intended to question Oriel Stewart again at the earliest possible opportunity.

★ ★ ★

Peace below stairs did not last for long. Next morning Mrs. Greene and Gertrude came to me in a fine fluster, reciting fresh and more startling incidents. Footsteps when no one was there; a gale blowing through the buttery on a calm June morning; a sack of potatoes exploding like a cannon and scattering themselves all over the kitchen floor.

'The servants won't stay, Miss Selina, not even the village girls.' Mrs. Greene folded her hands over her stomach in a gesture of determination. 'Not a minute more, they say, unless she goes.'

'She?' I stared at the housekeeper. 'Whom do you mean?'

'Why, Bethia Tudball, of course. She's the one what's doing this, Miss, and no mistake about it.'

'Bethia Tudball?' I glanced at Gertrude in amazement. 'You can't be serious, Mrs. Greene. That child? Why, she isn't capable of doing such things, and she's only just arrived.'

'Exactly.' Mrs. Greene pressed the point home in triumph. 'We didn't have nothing going on like this before she got here.'

'But she looks so . . .'

'They always do.'

I must have looked blanker than ever, for suddenly Mrs. Greene's umbrage evaporated, and she gave me a sympathetic look.

'Not met anything like this before, have you, Miss Selina? Well, that's natural enough, but I have. I've heard of goings-on of this sort, and it's always when there's a young girl about the place. Someone like Bethia. Haven't you looked at her eyes?'

'Well . . . yes . . . but . . .'

'Cunning, that's what they are. Sly and full of knowledge.'

'Gertie, do you think Mrs. Greene is

61

right?' I really didn't know what to say, for the housekeeper was quite correct. I hadn't had any previous experience of poltergeists or of strange young maids who could scare the wits out of their fellow-workers, yet I too had thought the girl's eyes were sly. 'You think it is Bethia?'

Gertie grunted.

'Looks like it. Mrs. G. is right; the girl's a crafty one, and until she got here, things were quiet enough. I remember when I was a lass something like this happened in a house where I was in service, just before I came to look after you. There was a wench like Bethia; young and seemingly dull of wits, but right down evil when it came to it.'

'If she doesn't go,' began Mrs. Greene, but I held up my hand.

'Very well, she shall go. I'll speak to Miss Oldfield when she calls to-day. She must try to find the child another position, and you'd better get a girl from the village to take her place.'

When I broke the news to Chloe of the failure of our experiment, she did not seem at all put out. Her eyes wrinkled at the corners, a smile touching her mouth.

'Poor Selina. Never mind, we must try something else.'

'She must go to-day, Chloe, or I shall lose the rest of my staff.'

'Of course.' Chloe took her cup, still faintly amused. 'I'll take her with me. Don't worry.'

With the problem of the extraordinary Bethia Tudball out of the way, I related to Chloe my meeting with Oriel and Marcus Tarrant.

'She is lovelier than I had expected,' I said finally, 'but people are right in what they say. She is just like a small child.'

Chloe snorted inelegantly.

'A child who should have a good spanking. Marcus spoils her, as I told you before. He would put her in a glass case if he could.'

'Yet she seems to roam about the meadows and woods without supervision.'

'Well, I suppose he can't spend every minute of each day watching her, and no doubt his staff are tired of trying to keep her indoors. Besides, why shouldn't she roam if she wants to?'

'Some harm might come to her.'

'Not to Oriel: she bears a charmed life.' Chloe was caustic. Then she said off-handedly: 'And what did you make of Marcus?'

'I thought him excessively rude,' I said shortly. 'I could have been a serf the way

63

he spoke to me, and at one point I thought he was going to hit me.'

Chloe chuckled.

'He's quite capable of doing so, I assure you. You had a lucky escape. I hope he didn't get it all his own way.'

'He did not.' I could hear the resentment in my own voice. 'I gave him as good as he gave me, and I'm determined to question that girl again. I'm sure she knows what I'm talking about.'

'Why are you still worrying about that old letter your aunt wrote to you years ago?' Chloe selected a chocolate biscuit and looked at me quizzically. 'It has become a positive obsession with you, and I really can't think why after all this time. Nothing happened here. If it had, I can assure you that Mrs. Cartwright would have given you every last detail, for she's a nosey old besom. The Misses Fanshawe would have known too; they are not much better when it comes to prying into things which don't concern them.'

'Then why did Oriel Stewart cry in that way? She wasn't crying before I mentioned the incident.'

'There wasn't an incident, and as to why Oriel started to cry, that's no mystery. She often cries for no reason. As I've said before,

Marcus should have her locked up.'

'Oh no!' Having met Oriel I couldn't accept Chloe's harsh judgment. 'She's a sweet thing. It would be cruel to put her into one of those dreadful homes for the insane. She isn't really mad, you know; just retarded. She wouldn't harm anyone.'

'How do you know?' The violet eyes were as hard as stones. 'You've only met her once.'

'But what could she do? How could she injure anyone? All she wants to do is to dance and play with her dolls.'

'And waste Marcus Tarrant's life for him.'

That was the nub of it, of course, and I sighed. Chloe was soured because of the attention bestowed on Oriel by the man she loved; the man who would probably never see her properly while he had to care for his ward.

'Take no notice of me.' Chloe must have seen the expression on my face, for her ire disappeared as quickly as it had come. 'Yes, she's probably harmless enough, as you say, but take my advice and don't ask her any more questions. If you do, Marcus may really take his crop to you.'

'He wouldn't dare.'

'Wouldn't he though! I've told you just how capable he is of doing so. Be sensible, love; keep away from Oriel.' Chloe rose to her feet with a sigh. 'Well, I must be on my way. Will you have Bethia taken to my carriage?'

'Of course, and I'm sorry that this should have happened, but Mrs. Greene and the others are so certain that she was responsible.'

Again that faint, satirical smile.

'Don't worry about it. There are other ways of dealing with the situation. I'll take my wicked protégée away, and you can live in peace again. We are dining with you to-morrow night, aren't we? David and I?'

'Yes, and Anthony. I look forward to it.'

She brushed my cheek with her lips, and I could smell the strong, musky perfume she used.

'Then until to-morrow. Take care, Selina; you see what a dangerous world we live in.'

★ ★ ★

I was very proud of my table on the following night. The damask cloth was without a blemish, the exquisite china and shimmering glass reflecting the light of the candles in tall silver holders. The meal was perfection too, and Anthony gave a deep sigh as he finished a piece of Stilton cheese.

'I don't think I shall dine with you again, coz,' he said and grinned at me. 'I shall get too fat for my little cottage.'

'Is it too small?' I was suddenly anxious, for I still had feelings of guilt about my cousin. 'Should I look for something else for you?'

'Of course not: I'm teasing you.' His voice was warm and reassuring. 'You've been most generous, and I'm grateful for the extra furniture you sent to me.'

'It was doing no good in the attic here.' I spoke humbly, for I could not rid myself of the thought that I ought to do more. 'If there is anything else you need . . .'

'Nothing at all, except a glass of old auntie's excellent brandy.'

Ignoring convention, we all moved into the drawing-room together, where Jessie served coffee and liqueurs, with brandy in huge glasses like balloons.

'I hear that you've quite fallen in love with the waxworks, Selina.'

I looked at David guardedly.

'Fallen in love with them? I don't understand.'

'Well, the Mouse tells me you go up to the gallery every day. I thought at first you had some reservations about them, but it seems that I was wrong.'

I cursed the Mouse for gossiping about what I did, but I was cool enough as I replied.

'Oh yes, I go and look at them from time to time.'

'Every day, Isa says.'

Chloe this time, smiling enigmatically over the rim of her glass.

'Well . . . yes . . . I suppose it is every day. You recall that Aunt Cassie stated in her Will that she wanted me to care for them.'

'Isa does that. You just look at them.'

Anthony laughed.

'But only in the daylight, I'll warrant.'

I turned my head swiftly.

'In the daylight? Of course in the daylight. What do you mean?'

'He means that besotted though you appear to be with Cassie's waxworks, you wouldn't dare go into the gallery at midnight.'

'Oh yes I would, if I had to.' I was not going to let Chloe see my sudden spurt of fear. 'What is the difference between noon and midnight?'

'All the difference in the world.' Stannard was cradling the brandy glass between his hands, savouring its aroma. 'The mind can play remarkable tricks in the dark. I doubt if you'd like it up there at night.'

'I'm sure I shouldn't mind at all,' I

lied quickly, knowing full well that my daytime quivers would become something like convulsions if I had to enter the gallery when the daylight had gone. 'After all, they are only waxworks.'

My bravado was sadly misplaced, for Chloe gave a gurgle of laughter.

'A challenge then, Selina. A wager that you will not go up there to-morrow night at twelve o'clock and stay for fifteen minutes.'

My throat was suddenly constricted as I looked round at their faces. Anthony was watching me with faint amusement; David somewhat more speculatively. Chloe was merely gloating because she knew she had me cornered. For all my affection for Chloe Oldfield, I could not escape the truth that there was within her a certain streak amounting almost to unkindness.

'Very well.' I was proud that my voice was so steady. 'You will accept my word that I remain there for a quarter of an hour?'

'Of course. We trust you implicitly, darling.' Chloe looked innocent. 'What shall the wager be?'

'I can't offer more than five pounds.' Anthony was regretful. 'And that will be a struggle.'

I tried to ignore what seemed to me a somewhat pointed reminder of our respective positions, and said hastily:

'Well, not money then. Anthony, you said you wanted me to sit for you. I'm not sure that I want to sit for anyone, but if I fail my test, you shall have your way. If I win, you will not mention the matter again. Is it a bargain?'

'Excellent.' Stannard was lighting a cigar. 'A most sensible solution. Midnight to-morrow then, and we shall call on you on the following morning to see whether you stayed the course, or whether Anthony will imprison you on canvas for posterity.'

I was glad when the subject was changed; even gladder when they bade me good-night and left, for then I could go to my room and confess my foolishness to Gertrude.

'I'll come with you,' she said promptly. 'I won't have you going up there at night with them devilish things. You shouldn't show off so, Miss Selina.'

'I know,' I was sadly chastened, 'but you can't come with me, Gertie. That would be cheating. I must go alone.'

'You shouldn't have agreed.'

'I couldn't help it after I had said . . . '

'Mm. Just so. Let this be a lesson to you to watch that pride of yours in future.' Gertrude picked up the hairbrush. 'Well, come along then; let's get on with putting you to bed.'

At twelve o'clock on the following night I went up to the gallery, candle in hand. I had never felt so nervous in all my life, nor more conscious that my predicament had been brought about by my own stupidity. Why hadn't I confessed straight away that I didn't want to come up here once the daylight had gone? The others might have teased me for cowardice, but at least I should be tucked up in my bed by now and not opening the gallery door, hearing it creak in a way I'm sure it never did by day.

I held the candle up, pausing for a moment or two until my eyes adjusted to the gloom. Then I moved forward, my heart thumping intolerably.

For a while I stayed with Henry VIII and Elizabeth, for I was growing more used to them. The light flickered over their waxen faces, their bodies looking larger than I remembered them. I thought there was even a hint of a smile on Gloriana's face, but that wasn't possible. The figure had not been designed with an amused look; rather to the contrary.

Finally I plucked up enough courage to move off. The prisoners in the Newgate cell looked quite awful, crouched by the bars,

71

staring blindly up at me. I shuddered, and swung round suddenly because I thought I had heard an unexpected noise. But there was nothing there. Just the silence swamping me, and the dim light casting grotesque shadows on the wall.

I made myself stop by the old ladies round the table. One held some embroidery in her stiff fingers, another a piece of knitting. I wished then that two of them really were the Misses Fanshawe, for nervous though the sisters were, they would at least have been some company for me.

To break the spell which seemed to be binding itself about me, I went into the workroom, but the plaster casts of the heads ranged round the shelves sent fresh shudders through me. They made me think of further tales the Mouse had told of the famous Madame Tussaud, who, in her youth, had fashioned the death-masks of those executed during the Terror in France. I had a horrific mental picture of her holding the severed head of Charlotte Corday in her lap, and left hastily, walking back to the main gallery.

Again I thought I heard something, nearly jumping out of my skin as I whirled about. Everything was just as before; still and silent.

Inevitably, I found myself at last beside the

gipsies. For a moment or two I concentrated hard on the two men and three women sitting on the ground round their camp fire. Then I pulled myself together, angered by my own timidness. I walked boldly forward and stared at the gipsy boy, meeting the black, unwinking eyes, my chin held high.

What it was about this particular figure which disturbed me so, I just could not tell. It was small enough not to be a threat, and the face was quite beautiful. I could feel perspiration on my brow, knowing the taper was quivering in my hand, making the flame play on the model and adding to its reality.

Finally he won, and I walked away, certainly not daring to turn back to look at him. I glanced at the watch pinned to my gown. Another seven minutes to go. I couldn't believe that I had been in the gallery for so short a while, for it felt like a lifetime. Off I went again, back to Henry, fashioned on Holbein's painting of him, keeping my eyes fixed on the sturdy legs and slashed shoes studded with gems.

When I heard the noise for the third time I knew I was not mistaken, and my voice was like an old woman's as I called out.

'Who is it? Is anyone there? Isa, is it you?'

There was no response, but I couldn't just stand there. I crept towards the end of the room from whence the sound had come.

'Isa? Are you there?'

My voice seemed to echo through the gallery, and I swallowed hard. It was no good. I should have to go, and admit my defeat to my friends in the morning. Anthony would have his own way, and I should have to sit for him. I simply couldn't stay there another second. I hurried in the direction of the door, and then stopped dead in my tracks, my hand over my mouth.

The gipsy boy had moved. My eyes widened in terror, and I could feel a trickle crawl down my spine. He had turned round and was now facing the opposite way. I tried to tell myself I was wrong; that he had always been placed as he was now, but it was no good. I had looked at him too often to be mistaken. Whilst I had been at the other end of the gallery, he had shifted his position and now had his back to me.

I let out a small moan, making for the door. I was still some way from it when I saw a movement in front of me. I almost dropped the candlestick and my legs wouldn't function. It must be nerves: nothing could have moved. No wonder my mocking friends had jumped on my conceit; I deserved it. The place was terrifying at night.

Then I saw the movement again, and forced myself to raise the light. For a whole second I saw her. An elderly woman with grey hair curled up at the back of her head; tall, with rather broad shoulders, in a lilac-coloured gown. She was quite near to me now, and I could see the dark eyes fixed on me.

'Aunt Cassie?' It was a mere thread of a sound. 'It . . . can't be . . . but . . . is it you?'

At that moment I felt a gust of wind coming from somewhere, and my candle blew out. I wanted to scream and run, but I didn't know what it was ahead of me, and so I fumbled in my pocket for the lucifers which I had had the good sense to bring with me.

How I got the candle alight again I shall never know. Kneeling on the floor, I struggled blindly with the box of matches, my fingers shaking so hard that I wasted three before the wick began to burn again. I dreaded standing up, but I had to, and when I was upright once more the figure had gone.

I could feel goose-pimples all over me, quickly checking my watch. It was a quarter past twelve, and my ordeal was over. I stumbled to the door, shutting it thankfully behind me, running downstairs as fast as I could.

Back in my bedroom, I lit every gasolier and lamp I could find, sitting on the edge of my bed and shaking from head to foot. I had told Gertie to go to bed and not to wait up for me: now I wished with all my heart that she was there, so that I could hold her hand in my icy one, and tell her what I had seen.

But I had just enough pride left not to go into the dressing-room where she slept. If I did go, she would comfort me, of course, but she would also scold me again. Furthermore, she would never believe that I had seen Aunt Cassie, and now, in my well-lit bedroom, I was beginning to think I hadn't seen her either.

How could I possibly have done so? I clenched my hands, thinking back for a second or two to that fearful moment. It was imagination, of course. Pure nerves and the darkness which had conjured up a ghost for me.

I did consider that perhaps someone had been playing a trick on me to make sure that I lost my bet, but I dismissed that quickly. Only Isa and I had keys to the gallery and the back door to the workroom, and not even

Anthony would break in and scare me half to death, simply because he wanted to paint me. Besides, the door had been securely locked when I first got there; no one had been in the gallery then.

I got up and looked in the mirror. My face was like chalk, my lips bleached. Much as I had dreaded the idea of going to the gallery at night, I had had no idea that it would be so bad. But now it was over, and when the others came on the following morning I would be calm and collected, assuring them that I had spent my alloted span with the waxworks.

I certainly would not mention the gipsy boy who had turned round when I wasn't looking, nor the apparition which had seemed so like the painting of Aunt Cassie.

I had won my wager, at a price, and that was that. I undressed quickly, turned out the lights and got into bed. Then, to my everlasting shame, I burst into tears, and had to hide my head under the pillow in case my sobs reached the ears of Gertie in the adjoining room.

4

The next morning I received the congratulations of Chloe and Anthony. David had been called away to see a patient, but Chloe hugged me, and Anthony sighed.

'I'm sorry you won, coz. I will keep my promise and not pester you again to sit for me, but it is such a waste. You are exquisite; far lovelier than your mother, to judge by her portrait.'

'Perhaps I may relent one day.' I had recovered most of my confidence by now, convincing myself that much of what I thought I had seen had been pure imagination brought about by the atmosphere and my own jumpy nerves. 'We'll see.'

'You're very brave.'

Anthony's voice was softer, and I gave him a quick glance. The dark blue eyes were almost serious for once.

'Not many women could have stood that.'

When they had gone, I made myself return to the gallery. As I went upstairs, I thought about Anthony's words. There had been something in the tone of his voice which I hadn't understood. It was rather more than admiration, but I soon forgot all about it as I reached the gallery.

In the sunlight I was as bold as brass as I walked slowly between the still figures, looking each one of them straight in the eye to shew how little I cared about them. The gipsy boy was round the right way again, but even that did not alarm me now. Of course he had always been round the right way; the rest was a fantasy on my part.

It was then that I had a remarkable piece of luck. In a drawer of a desk in the workroom, I found a bundle of notes about the gipsies in Cassie's handwriting. She had not attempted to write a flowing history, and some of the lines were too brief for so enthralling a subject. Rather, she seemed to have prepared an *aide memoire*, possibly to help her with her sketches and her directions to the now-departed Mr. Porter. Yet in between the facts, she had inserted one or two personal observations, cramming as many words as she could on to each page. I sat down and began to read.

I learned that gipsies were a people who had come originally from the Orient; that true Roms, or Romanies, were of pure blood, and contemptuous of others of their kind with mixed pedigrees. For a Romany to marry a non-Romany was to commit a mortal sin and to be cast out of the community, a fate which obviously had been regarded as far worse than mere death. '*Posh-rat*, the offspring of a Romany and a *gaujo*, or non-gipsy,' my aunt had written. 'Poor things: just half-breeds.' Of less account still, it seemed, was a *didakai*, the issue of a *posh-rat* and a non-gipsy.

Their occupations were many and varied, but horse-coping the most common. 'Horse-stealing more common still, but who can blame them?' Cassie had been tolerant over this lapse. 'They are normally peaceable beings,' she had gone on, 'but they have long memories and will fight well to defend themselves. This is admirable, as courage always is.'

Then there was a short note about their language. 'No alphabet: they don't write. Always stories and legends passed down by word of mouth, generation to generation. Signs left, which only other Romanies understand.' It appeared that as the gipsies wandered through the countryside, they left leaves, branches, coloured cloth and other items, which would mean nothing to any but the next Romany tribe which passed that way. It was a kind of code, known as *patrin*.

I turned the page and discovered that each

family had a leader. 'Eldest man chief: called *kako*, or uncle. How quaint, yet real power lies with the *phui dai*, or old woman, whom the Romanies called *bibi*, or auntie. She rules, advises, guides. Very wise: women so much more sensible than men.'

I smiled to myself. Obviously Cassie had not thought much of the male sex.

'Tight-knit families,' she had gone on. 'If anything happens to one member, all are affected. The death of one, a great tragedy to them all. We could learn much from them.'

Then there was a page devoted to the method of washing clothes and utensils some of which the Romanies regarded as clean, and others described as unclean. 'Not dirty,' my aunt had been at pains to emphasize, 'but ritually unclean, or *mókada*.'

I chuckled at the next part. Women, apparently, had always covered their legs with long skirts, presumably so that their menfolk should not become too excited by the sight of a shapely calf, and there was little prostitution amongst the girls; despite their charms. 'They never unbind their hair or comb it in the presence of men. Very right and proper,' wrote Cassie, 'one cannot be too careful.'

There was a list of Romany words Cassie

81

had collected, such as *chavo*, meaning boy, and *vardo*, for a waggon. There were details of the herbs they used to cure sickness, and a string of typical Romany names.

'Camps may seem disorganised, but they are not. *Bibi* sees to that. Proud that none can understand their jargon: if only I could. If they would open their hearts to us, we should learn so much. How I wish . . . '

The notes stopped abruptly and I frowned. What had Cassie wished? Clearly, she had been fascinated by the Romanies and not only, I suspected, because she wished to make wax models of them. They had caught her imagination, sucking her into their mysterious web, but she was a *gaujo*, always to be left outside their magic circle.

When I finally decided to go and talk to the Romanies, I felt confident that Aunt Cassie's notes had given me some insight into their ways, but as soon as I left the grounds and approached their encampment, I knew I was wrong. A few pages of scrappy writing were not enough to breach the wide gulf between us.

When I got nearer to the waggons I could see how well-cared for they were. The varnish on them was fresh, the brasswork had been rubbed until it seemed like gold. Black leather was polished so that it looked wet and shiny: the trace-chains of the harnesses were silver-bright.

At the time of my visit there were five adults present, a few children playing on the grass some way away. The two younger men were not tall: rather slender with swarthy complexions and hair as dark as pitch. Their brown eyes were clear but very watchful. There was one girl sitting cross-legged by the fire. She was about eighteen, with a deep olive-coloured skin, rosy cheeks and sparkling eyes. All wore ear-rings, the women sporting many necklaces and bangles, with gaily coloured scarves round their heads.

An elderly woman was sitting on the steps of one of the waggons, and through its open door I could see a single room, furnished with small, built-in cupboards and lockers, and a two-tiered bed arrangement.

There was a long silence between us, broken only by the crackle of the fire. When it was clear that they were not going to make the first overture, I said hesitantly:

'Good-morning. I am Selina Rochford, and I live at Steeple Court. I hope I am not disturbing you.'

At first there was no reaction. They simply went on staring at me, and so I tried again.

'Please . . . I mean you no harm. I have come to ask for your help.'

I looked at the eldest of the three men. He had grizzled hair, a suit with stovepipe trousers, leather waistcoat, and a scarlet kerchief round his throat. I thought he must be the *kako* to whom Cassie had referred, and so I addressed myself to him.

'Will you help me?'

My aunt's belief that the eldest female held greatest sway in the family was soon confirmed, for he turned to the woman on the steps, shrugging his shoulders. She was smoking a clay pipe, regarding me without fear, but still with some suspicion. Finally, she spoke.

'Help, Missie? What help can we give you?'

'I'm not sure. Perhaps none, but I wanted to ask you some questions.'

The man said something in a tongue which I did not understand, but the *bibi*, as I took her to be, waved him to silence.

'We know nothing,' she said. 'What could we tell you?'

She was not encouraging, but now that I was there, I was determined to try to get something from them.

'I don't know, but let me ask you. I believe you come here every year.'

The *bibi* and the grey-haired man exchanged a look.

84

'What if we do?'

'No reason at all.' I was quick to reassure them. 'Indeed, why shouldn't you come? No, it was simply that I had been told you visited Leyden for a few weeks and always at this time of year.'

'We are not on your land.' The man's hostility was growing. 'Why do you bother us?'

'Please!' I held out a conciliatory hand. 'I am not trying to harass you in any way, and I know that you are not trespassing. That isn't why I have come. It is because I want to know what happened here in the village some fifteen years ago. That is when you first came to Leyden, isn't it?'

There was a sudden and very definite change in the atmosphere, and for the first time I felt frightened. The *kako* was scowling, hands thrust into his pockets, and even the girl by the fire lowered her eyelids so that she seemed to shut herself off from me. But I wouldn't be beaten.

'I know something happened.' I said it crisply, to shew them I was not afraid of their menacing silence. 'My aunt wrote to me about it long ago, but she did not tell me what it was. Now she is dead, so I do not know what she meant, and none of her friends and acquaintances will admit that anything took place. They said that if it had, they would have known about it.'

Even to the Romanies, I would not mention Cassie's recent letter, using my small white lie as before.

'Well then.' The *bibi* took the pipe out of her mouth and grinned. I could see that she had only two or three teeth in her head, and somehow the grimace made me shiver. 'If that's what they say, why do you ask us?'

'Because I don't believe them. At least, I don't think they are actually lying . . . well . . . I hope they're not.' I hesitated. This was more difficult than I had imagined it would be. 'I think they are mistaken, and really do not know what it was. But my aunt was telling the truth; that I do know. Whatever it was, I believe it upset her very much, although she never spoke of it to a soul.'

'We have nothing to do with folk in the village or the big houses.' The *kako* was gruff. 'Them not like us; we not like them. Go away, Missie.'

'I will soon.' I stood my ground, and concentrated on the old woman. 'If my aunt's friends really are telling the truth, then whatever it was may have taken place elsewhere. I know my aunt . . . well . . . that is . . . I know she came to see you sometimes.'

86

'Never saw her.' The *bibi*'s grin was more pronounced. 'She wouldn't come here.'

I hesitated again. Perhaps the Romanies had been unaware of the careful watch which Cassie had kept on them, and it might be tactless to press the point. They might not like the notion of waxen images of themselves in the gallery at Steeple Court. Desperately, I tried another way.

'Please believe me when I say I am not trying to pry into your business: I would not do that. But why do you come here every year? Why have you come for the last fifteen years?'

By now, two more women and another man had strolled up to the waggons, moving closer to encircle me, and it needed a great deal of self-control not to take to my heels and run.

'That's our affair. We keep to ourselves and interfere with no one.'

'I know, I know!' I gave an impatient sigh. 'I've told you, I don't want to talk of your private business. I merely want to know what went on all those years ago, and why you come here, just for a few weeks in June.'

The *bibi* was watching me sombrely, the others moving in slightly. If I didn't run soon, I shouldn't have the chance later, and I was about to step back when the old woman said:

'You've got an honest face, my deari.' She gestured her family to retreat, which they did with prompt obedience. 'But our reasons for coming here have nothing to do with you. We are just waiting for something.'

'Waiting for something?' I was flabbergasted. 'You mean that you've been waiting for something for fifteen years?'

'Aye, that's right.' She took another puff at the pipe. 'Maybe we'll have to wait as long again. Who knows?'

'Could what you are waiting for have anything to do with what occurred? Might it be something connected with what my aunt wrote of?'

She shook her head, ear-rings jangling.

'Nay. What we wait for concerns no one but us.'

'I see.'

I knew that I was beaten, for neither the *bibi* nor any of the others would say any more.

'Thank you for talking to me,' I said finally. 'May I come and see you again?'

The *bibi* shrugged.

'If you want to, but we can't help you.'

'I'll come anyway. Thank you.'

I could feel eyes boring into my back as

I walked away, wondering if I would really have the courage to return. After all, what was the point if they would not help me? Yet someone must know what Cassie meant. She was a sensible woman and no romancer. There must be an answer somewhere, and I had to find it.

★ ★ ★

When I told Chloe about my visit to the gipsies, and how evasive they had been, she frowned.

'It was foolish of you to go,' she said shortly. 'They might have done anything to you. Everyone hates them coming here, but thank God they don't stay long. Really, Selina, why do you keep asking about this mythical occurrence? I doubt if you ever thought about it until you arrived here. You said you were only a child when your aunt wrote to you, and surely if it was something which mattered, she would have written to you again when you were older. Can't you forget it?'

'No, I can't.' I poured Chloe another cup of tea. 'Don't you think it is odd that the gipsies only started to come here at the very time when Aunt Cassie said something happened?'

'Not in the least; pure coincidence.'

'I don't think so. They said they were waiting for something. What could that possibly be?'

'Heaven knows! Does it matter? Really, you must . . .'

'Chloe, if you don't recall any incident in the village itself, or here at Steeple Court, was there anything which happened to the gipsies at that time?'

Chloe laughed, her impatience gone.

'Dearest, how persistent you are! And as to whether anything happened to those gipsies all that time ago, I haven't the faintest idea. I was only a child, and never allowed near their camp. The whole lot of them could have gone up in smoke, and I should have been none the wiser.'

I looked at her thoughtfully. She was right, of course. Children like Chloe Oldfield would never have had any contact with the Romanies.

'They're all alike. Dirty, shifty, untruthful and dishonest. Keep away from them, or you'll find yourself in trouble.'

Before I could tell Chloe that the Romanies were far from dirty, Jessie was at the drawing-room door to announce the arrival of Anthony. He strolled in, kissing Chloe's forehead and raising my hand to his lips.

'I have come to beg a cup of tea. Will you take pity on a starving artist?'

'Of course.' Again that pin-prick concerning his financial status, but perhaps I was being over-sensitive about it. Anthony was a born tease, and most of the time he didn't appear to care about money or possessions. 'Here you are, and some angel-cake to go with it.'

'Selina has been to see the gipsies.' Chloe was smiling blithely at my cousin. 'She thinks we might know why they come here every year. Why they have done so for the last fifteen years.'

Sewall finished his tea and put the cup down before he turned his head to look at me.

'No one ever knows why gipsies do anything. They take jolly good care that outsiders are kept in ignorance.'

'And as I have explained to Selina, when we were young, we were never allowed near them.'

Anthony nodded.

'True enough. Once or twice I sneaked down to have a look at them, but my father caught me in the end and thrashed me so hard I never tried again. Sweet love, do forget them, and this idiotic crusade you are waging on the part of the late lamented

91

Cassie. I'm sure you misunderstood her, for she never raised the subject again, did she? Life has much more to offer you than this. Shall I shew you what?'

'No thank you,' I replied, trying not to blush. 'I'm sorry if I'm being a bore.'

'You could never be that, but . . . '

'I'll try to forget it,' I lied quickly. 'Some more tea?'

After they had gone and Jessie had removed the tray, I sat and thought about Cassie's recent letter. I was probably on the wrong track about the Romanies' connection, for it was obvious that they had not seen her watching them, and she had not mentioned anything amiss in the notes which I had found. She had shewn no fear of them and seemed to admire them, so it must be something quite different which had worried her so. Perhaps it was something connected with the missing jewellery, but for how long had it been missing? It would be difficult to find out, since Cassie so seldom wore any of it.

I sighed in sheer disappointment. In spite of my initial determination to find the cause of Cassie's misery, I had made no progress at all, and now I was beginning to wonder if I ever would. It was a disheartening thought.

* * *

I woke that night quite suddenly, sitting bolt upright in bed. I was sure that I had heard a noise, but when I lit my bedside candle and looked at the clock I saw it was two a.m. No one would be about at that time of night; it must have been a dream. I was just about to lie down again when I heard the sound once more and got up, slipping on my robe.

The candle wavered as I walked out into the dark corridor. It was quite deserted and so were the stairs as I descended them carefully. I looked round the hall, into the drawing-room, dining-room, and library. There was nothing to be seen. I shrugged and began to mount the stairs. Then it came again, this time from overhead. The gallery? I shivered and quickened my step, shutting my door firmly behind me. If the noises had come from the gallery, I was certainly not going to investigate. I had had enough of those waxworks after dark.

The next morning I questioned Mrs. Greene, Jessie, Nell, and finally Isa Hedley. They all denied hearing a sound, each insisting that they had been fast asleep in their beds, looking at me as though I were weak in the head.

When I met Gertrude in the passage I

asked the same question, and much to my surprise, and considerable relief, she nodded.

'Yes, I did hear something. Don't know what time it was, but latish.'

'What sort of sound did you think it was, Gertie?'

'Don't really know. Like a creaking noise, I thought.'

'Yes, that's what I thought too.'

'Didn't anyone else hear it?'

'It seems not, or at least they say not.'

'Probably nothing.' Gertie had three of my dresses over her arm which she had been pressing in the sewing-room downstairs. 'Old houses make funny noises at night. Shouldn't worry about it if I was you. I expect I was wrong about what I thought I heard and saw too, for that matter.'

'Gertie!' I was alarmed. 'You didn't tell me you had seen anything.'

'Well, I didn't want to scare you.' She was trying to avoid my accusing eyes. 'But I got up and lit a candle. Looked out of my door too, and saw someone in the passage.'

'But who was it?' I asked impatiently. 'Gertie, for heaven's sake, whom did you see?'

'Well that's the queer thing. I could have sworn it was . . . '

'Miss Selina.'

I started as Jessie Trent appeared at my elbow, turning sharply, my voice somewhat curt.

'Yes, yes, Jessie, what is it?'

'Dr. Stannard's here. He'd like to see you.'

'Tell him I will come down in a moment or two.'

'No, you go now, Miss Selina,' said Gertrude, and began to move towards my bedroom. 'I'll hang these up, and we'll talk again later.'

I was very reluctant to break off the conversation at so tantalizing a point, but Gertie had now disappeared, and I didn't want Jessie to start asking herself questions.

When I had finished with David, who wanted nothing more important than my assurance that I would attend a garden party in aid of his pet charity, I hurried upstairs again to find Gertie. She wasn't in my bedroom, nor in the dressing-room where she still slept.

At first I was not worried. Obviously Gertie would not sit about with folded hands, waiting for my visitor to go, and I went down to the sewing-room, expecting to find her at work on more gowns. But she wasn't there either, nor was she in the

95

kitchen, or in any of the lower rooms.

I summoned Mrs. Greene and Jessie and demanded that they help me to find her. Jessie called to Nell Foster to join in the search, and for nearly an hour we looked over the house and in the gardens, but there was no sign of Gertie.

'I don't understand it,' I said, as we gathered in the kitchen again. 'Where on earth can she be?'

'Perhaps Miss Hedley knows.' Mrs. Greene looked faintly worried now. 'I've just seen her come down from the gallery. Could Gertie have gone up there, do you think?'

'I doubt it, but it's possible. Nell, fetch Miss Hedley, will you?'

Isa came into the kitchen with small, scuttling steps, looking as nervous as ever. She shook her head at once when I asked my question.

'Oh no! I would never allow anyone into the gallery without your consent, Miss Rochford, not even Gertrude. I haven't seen her since early this morning.'

'This is ridiculous!'

My irritation was fostered by an uneasiness which was growing by the minute. Why on earth should Gertie suddenly disappear, particularly as we had arranged to have another talk as soon as David had gone?

For a second something unpleasant flickered through my mind. Gertie had been on the point of telling me whom she had seen in the passage, and from the way that she had spoken, it seemed to me it was a person she had not expected to find there. I shook myself. I was growing fanciful again.

'She can't be far off,' I said firmly. 'We must have another look. What about the wash-house. Did you look there, Nell?'

'Yes, Miss. She weren't there.'

'Could she have gone to the village?' Mrs. Greene was growing as troubled as I by now. 'She made no mention that she was going out, but that's not to say she didn't go.'

'No, of course not.' I sighed with relief. 'That's the answer, I'm sure. I expect she'll be back shortly. I'll be in the sitting-room. Ask her to see me as soon as she comes in.'

But Gertie didn't come in, and in another two hours I had organised a further search, including the main cellars and outhouses, all to no avail.

I was really worried now. It was so unlike Gertie to behave in this fashion that I could not get it out of my head that something had happened to her.

It was five in the afternoon when Mrs. Greene came to me with a note in her hand.

'Nell has just found this in Gertie's room, Miss Selina. It was tucked behind her clock and we didn't see it before. It wasn't in an envelope, and so we read it.'

I took the paper from her. It was a brief message, with Gertie's name at the bottom.

'Sorry to go off without speaking to you, Miss Selina,' it said, 'but I had a message from the village that my aunt was ill and I've gone to see her. Don't think I've mentioned her to you, but she lives not far away. I must go.'

'But this isn't Gertie's writing,' I said quickly. 'I'm sure it isn't.'

'Nell thought it was.' Mrs. Greene looked at me dubiously. 'She shewed me a list of linen which Gertie had wanted. Looked the same to me.'

'Let me see it, and bring Nell back with you.'

I waited like a cat on hot bricks until the housekeeper returned with Nell, who was bridling because her word had been doubted. I looked at the list which Gertie had given to Nell, and then at the note. Certainly the handwriting looked identical.

'Are you sure you're not mistaken, Miss Selina?' asked Mrs. Greene after a slight pause. 'It does look like Gertie's hand, doesn't it?'

'Yes it does,' I said slowly, 'and come to think of it, of course, I haven't seen much of Gertie's writing. In fact, probably none at all. We've never had cause to write to one another, you see. We've always been there to talk about whatever it was we wanted to say.'

Nell sniffed indignantly, and I smiled apologetically.

'I'm sorry, Nell. I didn't mean to doubt you, but . . .'

'That's all right, Miss.'

Nell was mollified, and went off about her business, but I still could not really accept what had happened. I had known Gertie all my life, and we had had no secrets. Why, then, had she never mentioned her aunt to me?

'Will that be all, Miss Selina?'

'Yes thank you, Mrs. Greene, but when someone goes to the village ask them to find out if they can where Gertie's aunt lives.'

'Be difficult.' Mrs. Greene pursed her lips. 'We don't know her name, do we?'

'If it was Gertie's aunt on her father's side, it will be Jennings, unless, of course, she was married.'

Questions were duly asked, but no answers were forthcoming. Clearly Gertie's mysterious relation did not live in Leyden itself, and it might be in any one of a dozen surrounding hamlets that she resided. I attended to my own toilet, refusing Jessie's offer of assistance. I had grown too used to Gertrude to want anyone else performing such intimate tasks for me.

Nothing happened for the next two days, but on the third a boy came up from the village with another letter, in the same handwriting, which he said a woman had given to him, although he could not describe her appearance.

This time the note was longer and more shattering. Gertie, it seemed, had decided not to return. Her aunt was moving south, where the air suited her better, and Gertie was going with her.

I would not let Mrs. Greene see my anxiety, nor the unshed tears behind my eyes, but when I was alone again I read the missive with more care. Certainly it was phrased as Gertie would have spoken, and why should Nell lie about Gertie's handwriting? Yet, equally, why should Gertie suddenly desert me after so many years, not even troubling to come and talk to me about her departure, but simply relying upon two letters to sever a connection between us which I imagined to be unbreakable?

I went to my room to weep, for my sorrow

was a very private thing. I felt totally lost, as if part of myself had gone, wondering if Gertie would ever come back, or even trouble to write again.

Now I should never know what it was that she had been going to tell me. I should never learn who it was whom Gertie had seen that night in the corridor.

I think it was then that the first suspicion struck me; like a heavy thud between the shoulder blades.

Was it merely a coincidence that now I should never find out who had been up and about that night, or was it something more sinister? Gertie and I had been talking in the passage that morning; anyone could have overheard us, apart from Jessie, who had come to announce the arrival of David Stannard.

I tried to tell myself that I was being melodramatic, and was only letting my mind wander along such an unpleasant path because my conceit had received so sharp a blow. Gertie had thought it more important to go with her ailing relation than to stay with me, and so I looked for some outlandish reason for denying this truth.

Or was it the truth? Had Gertie really gone of her own free will, or had someone wanted to stop her from telling me about the night-walker? It was a terrible thought, but I could not get it out of my head, yet nor could I speak of my suspicions to anyone else. It was the kind of confidence I had reserved for Gertie alone.

For the moment I would have to accept the whole affair on its face value, and when Chloe expressed surprise at my maid's abrupt departure, I was able to say in the most unemotional of voices that such things sometimes happened.

'I should be furious,' said Chloe, indignant on my behalf. 'I should want to give her a piece of my mind for behaving so thoughtlessly.'

'But I don't know where she is.'

Chloe gave me a meditative look, then she shook her head.

'No, I suppose not. In fact, no one knows where she is, do they?'

5

Despite my unhappiness at Gertrude's departure, I did not let myself forget my original reason for coming to Leyden, and when Chloe told me that Marcus Tarrant had gone away for two days, I decided to take the golden opportunity of talking to Oriel again.

It seemed like a form of cruelty to torment the girl, but I was so convinced that she must know something, that I stifled my conscience and set out for The Grange. If she had been entirely ignorant of the subject we had discussed at our first meeting, why had she been so distressed? Somehow I could not accept that dissolving into a paroxysm of tears was the normal pattern of behaviour for Oriel. It had to be something more than that.

I found her in the gardens of The Grange, thankful that I should not have to invade Tarrant's house in his absence. The grounds were even more extensive than those of Steeple Court, and I walked some way before I came upon Oriel floating back and forth on a swing which had been strung between two sturdy trees.

I held back for a moment before she saw me, watching the fluid movement of her body, the perfection of neck and jaw as she flung her head back, laughing to herself with sheer delight. It was more difficult than ever to remember that this marvellously formed being, with all the rich invitation of womanhood, was a mere babe when it came to matters of the mind. It was more than sad; it was a ludicrous and spiteful trick of Nature, and I wondered what Marcus Tarrant made of it.

I paused to consider whether he loved her; not just affectionately, as a guardian would cherish his ward, but as a woman. Would he care that she played with dolls, when he looked at the line of her long, slim legs, now kicking her skirts free as she soared into the air.

The idea was oddly disturbing, but I told myself that I was merely thinking of Chloe Oldfield and her apparently hopeless passion for Tarrant. If there was more to my musings than that, I did not allow myself to dwell on it.

When Oriel saw me she cried out in welcome. It was obvious that she had completely forgotten our last encounter, and was simply glad to see someone in her shady paradise. I doubted very much if she remembered who I was, but I was wrong about that.

'Selina! You have come to see my dolls! Oh, how splendid. Wait, wait! I'll stop the swing and shew them to you.'

There was an adult's strength in the way she slowed the swing and leapt from the seat, holding out her hand to me.

'They're over here. Come and see.'

I followed obediently and gazed down at the row of dolls on a rustic seat under a willow tree. They were of all shapes and sizes: some china, some wax, some of wood, and three older rag dolls. I duly admired them as proudly Oriel shewed me how two of them could close their eyes, whilst another had real hair, each strand fixed carefully into the wax head.

'They are lovely,' I said, feigning interest as Oriel sat a china doll with an expensive silk dress back in its place. 'But they are all girls, aren't they? Have you no boy-dolls?'

Something passed over Oriel's face like a shadow.

'No, I don't like boys.'

'Don't you? Did you never have any boy playmates?'

'No! No!' She was almost angry now, picking up a shabby rag doll and holding

105

it against her as if it gave her comfort. 'I hate boys.'

'Even Marcus?' I asked softly. 'He's a boy, or at least, a man.'

The momentary passion was spent, and Oriel smiled again.

'Marcus is different. I love him, and he loves me.'

I didn't doubt it, and my tone was rather tart.

'Yes, I expect he does. See, I have brought you a present. Do you like sweets?'

'Oh yes!'

She was eager, almost snatching the candy-box from my hand, sinking to the grass as she opened it and selected a violet cream. I watched her stuff three or four more into her mouth, hoping she wouldn't be sick. Then I said gently:

'Tell me about your other toys, and what you do here at The Grange. Do you have lessons?'

She answered with her mouth full, a trickle of chocolate running down her chin.

'No, I don't like lessons.'

'Then what do you do?'

'I play with my dolls, and I've got a cardboard theatre too. I've got lots of toys. Do you want to see them?'

'Not now,' I replied hastily, wishing to

turn the inconsequential conversation into more serious channels. 'Do you remember we met before? I suppose you do, for you knew my name.'

'Oh yes.' She was looking at me a trifle warily now as her fingers groped for another candy. 'I can't remember what we talked about though.'

'Your dolls mostly.'

'Of course.' She was relieved at once. 'They're my best friends.'

'They, and Marcus?'

She giggled, and something behind that snigger was not childlike.

'On no, Marcus is not just a friend.'

I stiffened, but dropped the subject quickly.

'We also spoke of other things.'

'Did we?' She wasn't interested, too busy with a piece of nougat. 'We might have done.'

'I asked you whether you could recall something which happened here a long time ago. You said no, but I didn't believe you. I think you do know, and I want you to tell me what it was.'

The candy-box dropped to the grass, its contents forgotten as Oriel got to her feet. I had seen a number of emotions flit across her face that morning, including one which I had not liked at all, but now she was frightened again, and there was no mistaking it.

'I . . . I . . . don't know what you mean.'

'Yes you do,' I returned quietly. 'I'm sure you do. It's just that you don't want to tell me about it, but you must. It's so important.'

'No! No!' She was moving backwards now. 'Go away, go away! I don't want you here. You say horrid things to me.'

'I don't mean to.' I tried to soothe her; to stop her flight. 'I want us to be friends, Oriel, and I did bring you sweets, didn't I, and admired your dolls. I wouldn't have done that, if I'd wanted to hurt you.'

She paused, doubt clouding the vacant eyes once more.

'And I wouldn't ask you questions unless I had to, believe me. Please help me. What happened?'

'I . . . don't know . . . I don't know . . . go away . . . go away! I hate you!'

Her face was contorted with rage for a second, then she was in tears as before, racked with misery so deep that I felt more like a monster than ever.

'Please, Oriel, don't . . .'

But she was running back to the house, screaming as she went. I watched her with a sinking heart. Not only had I failed to get a single clue from her, but now Marcus Tarrant would hear of my visit. The servants would inform him of the state Oriel had been in, and doubtless Oriel herself would tell him I had been there. She would tell Marcus everything, like a small child confiding all her secrets as she snuggled up against him.

I cursed under my breath, and went back to Steeple Court to wait for the storm to break over my head.

* * *

It came the next day. I was in the morning-room, reading a book about wild flowers, when the door opened. Jessie Trent tried to announce my unexpected visitor, but Tarrant almost knocked her over as he strode past her and came to rest a few feet away from me.

'Thank you, Jessie,' I said with commendable calm. 'That will be all.'

She watched me with worried eyes, but I gave her a dismissive nod before looking back at Tarrant. He was in riding habit again, still carrying a crop. I wondered if he ever wore anything else, and wished fervently that he would leave his whip outside when he came visiting.

'Damn you,' he said furiously, before I could open my mouth. 'How dare you go to The Grange and upset Oriel again? Have you forgotten so soon what I said to you?'

'I have not.'

I refused to shew fear in the face of his anger, although it was rather terrifying, and every line round his mouth and between his brows warned me of my danger.

'You were trespassing.'

'As you are doing now,' I returned with spirit. 'I did not invite you here, Sir Marcus.'

'Nor did I invite you to The Grange.'

'Then it seems we are quits.'

'Indeed we are not.' The tawny eyes held mine, so that I felt like a trapped rabbit. 'I told you that you would answer to me if you went near Oriel again. Why did you do it? In the name of hell, why can't you leave the child alone?'

'Child?' I rose to my feet. 'Will you take sherry, Sir Marcus, or would you prefer something stronger?'

'Nothing, thank you,' he snapped. 'And yes, child. That's what she is.'

My smile was brief and bleak.

'Only in some things. If you believe otherwise, you are blind.'

The frown deepened, but some of his rage was dissipating now.

'I have no idea what you are talking about.'

110

'Haven't you? Think about it. Are you sure you would not like some refreshment?'

'No! I do not want sherry, whisky, brandy, or any other concoction you may wish to offer me. I simply want to know why you dared to come to my home and torment my ward.'

'You know why. I told you the last time.'

She knows nothing; she cannot remember. I told you that too — the last time.'

'Then if Oriel cannot help me, perhaps you can.' I sat down, concealing my shaking hands, for I was determined I would not let Tarrant see how he was affecting me. 'You have lived here all your life. If Oriel can't or won't, help me, perhaps you will. What happened here in Leyden years ago?'

'I haven't the faintest idea.' He slashed the crop against his riding boot. 'I was up at Oxford then. As I understand it, everyone has told you that nothing happened. Why, then, do you persist in your ridiculous questions?'

'Because my aunt was neither a nervous woman nor a fool,' I said quietly. 'She wrote to me when I was a child about this incident, but gave no details.'

'Your aunt was sick and old. Her mind was probably going.'

My lips curved in an unamused smile.

111

'Yes, that would be a very convenient explanation, wouldn't it, but I've just told you that she wrote to me many years ago, and she certainly wasn't senile then.'

It was a lie, of course, but Cassie had not wanted anyone to know about her recent letter sent to me in London. Besides, Marcus might well be the one whom Cassie had dreaded.

There was a brief pause. Then I said:

'The Romanies come here every year, always at this time. They have done so for the last fifteen years. Do you know why? Have you the answer to that question, if not my first?'

'Of course not.' He was scathing. 'Gipsies come and go at will. Who knows why they are in one place at one time, and in another at some other season? Talk sense, girl. And since we are speaking of these infernal gipsies, I'm told that you went to see them, and alone.'

'I did.'

'Then you're a bigger fool than I took you for.'

'And you're a bigger boor than I took you for.' I felt my colour rise at his insolence. 'Do you always address your hostess in such a tone?'

His laugh was short and sarcastic.

'You are not my hostess, as you reminded me just now. I am a trespasser, just like you, and don't change the subject. What made you take such a chance?'

'They did me no harm.'

'Then you were lucky.'

'And they were far more courteous than you, Sir Marcus.'

'For God's sake stop worrying about the niceties of convention, Miss Rochford, and pay attention to what I am saying. It is unsafe for a woman like you to go to their encampment alone. Why you should want to go at all is beyond me, but if you must behave like a cretin, then at least take your maid with you next time.'

I shall never know to this day why I said the next few words, for normally Marcus Tarrant was the very last person in whom I would choose to confide, but I could hear myself blurting them out before I could stop myself.

'My . . . my maid has gone.'

Something in my voice must have got through to Tarrant, for when I looked at his face again it was, for the first time, free from anger. Oh yes; Chloe was right. He was handsome. Damn Chloe; damn Oriel Stewart, and, most of all, damn Marcus Tarrant.

'Oh? Gone where?'

'I don't know . . . well . . . that is . . . I suppose I do.'

'You'd better tell me about it.'

I was going to say that it was none of his business, but something stopped me. His expression shewed no sign of interest, yet it was a relief to talk about it to someone, even if that person was not above suspicion. I explained what had happened, even the conversation which Gertie and I had had on the morning of her disappearance.

'I see.' He ran a speculative eye over me. 'Rather strange, I would say. What are you going to do about it?'

'Nothing, what can I do?' I was horrified to find that I was nearly in tears, quickly looking down at my lap. I should never be able to hold my head up again if Marcus Tarrant saw me crying. 'Gertrude has gone south with her aunt, and that is that. She may write to me again later.'

'And if she doesn't?'

'Then I shall know she does not intend to return to me, but proposes to make her home with her aunt.'

'Most inconvenient for you; it also sounds highly implausible.'

There was another uncomfortable pause. Then he said abruptly:

'Keep away from that encampment. It's not safe.'

'I wanted to ask them if they knew anything about what happened fif . . . '

'Christ! Not that again!' Tarrant was irritable once more. 'Chloe told me you were obsessional about it, and she was right. Everyone keeps telling you nothing happened. Why don't you believe them?'

'I don't know.' I wasn't quite ready to spit back at him yet, for the unshed tears had not completely gone. 'But I don't. At least, I believe them to be mistaken. Why should the Romanies suddenly start to come here every year since I received Aunt Cassie's letter? There must be some connection.'

Shaken as I was, I managed to keep up the pretence of the old letter.

'I have no idea, and I doubt if there is the slightest connection between the letter and those wanderers. How could there be? Use your common sense.'

'I'm trying to.' I lifted my chin, feeling secure enough to look him in the eye again. 'Please don't concern yourself with me. Unlike Oriel, I'm not a child.'

The thrust went home, and his lips thinned in anger.

'An unnecessary comment, Miss Rochford, but since you have raised the subject of my ward, let me repeat what I said before, and this is the last warning you will get. Leave her alone. Don't come to The Grange, or try to speak to her ever again. I will not have her worried and upset by a stupid female with no sense in her head. Do you understand me? Leave Oriel alone, or, by God, I'll make you do so.'

My own anger was roused again now. If Tarrant could be insufferable, so could I.

'You're very protective, Sir Marcus. Oriel is most fortunate to have such a devoted . . . friend?'

It was a suggestive sneer, and I meant it to be.

Tarrant took three steps across the floor and jerked me out of my chair. I could feel his fingers biting into my shoulders through the thin silk of my gown. He was hurting me, but that was not the reason why I was trembling.

'You're just as much a bitch as Chloe Oldfield,' he said through set teeth, 'but she knows better than to upset Oriel, and you'll learn the same lesson. Now bear that in mind; I shall not use words next time.'

And then he was gone. I had no chance to ring for Jessie to shew him out, for the door was slamming behind him and I had collapsed in my chair, shaking in every limb.

I suppose I had deserved what I got for my unpardonable comment, yet I was not going to be intimidated by Marcus Tarrant.

Oriel knew something; of that I was sure. What it was, and how I was going to make her divulge it, I had no idea, but I was going to try, no matter what Tarrant thought of me, nor what he would do to me when he discovered that I had ignored his instructions.

Suddenly I thought about Gertie again. If she had been here, I could have wept on her shoulder and told her what an unpleasant creature Tarrant was, but Gertie wasn't here. Only then did something else occur to me as a result of my disastrous discussion with Oriel's guardian. I still could not quite believe the tale of Gertrude and her aunt, and, on reflection, I don't think Tarrant did either.

I shivered. I wouldn't let myself think about it; the alternative was too dreadful to contemplate.

★ ★ ★

That night I lay awake for a long time. There were many things for me to consider and worry about, and a new and quite unexpected complication which I had not

117

thought to encounter. But I would be firm with myself; I would not let my thoughts wander in the direction of Marcus Tarrant.

It was when I was at last drifting towards sleep that I heard the noise again. For a moment I considered putting my head under the bedclothes and ignoring it. If I went out into the corridor, I might see whoever it was that Gertie had seen. Then I shook off my nervousness, put on a peignoir, lit a candle and opened the door. I had only gone a few steps when the flame flickered wildly and then went out.

I had not lived on an army post for twenty years for nothing, and my language was far from lady-like, although I kept my ripe oaths under my breath. I considered going back to my room to re-light the candle, but then decided to feel my way downstairs and get some matches from the kitchen instead.

I groped my way along the passage, my foot exploring the top stair. I had only taken about four steps, when I felt myself thrown out into space, rolling down the remainder of the flight and arriving at the bottom with a sickening thud. I think I cried out as I fell. Either that, or the noise of my descent, awoke Isa Hedley, who was first on the scene, and then the servants, for they came hurrying down from their attic bedrooms, lights in hand, clucking and exclaiming as they saw me lying helpless on the landing.

'Miss Selina!' Mrs. Greene quickly handed her candlestick to Jessie, and knelt beside me, raising me up. 'Whatever has happened?'

My ankle was hurting me and my whole body felt jolted by my tumble, but even so I managed to keep my voice dry.

'I think I have fallen downstairs, Mrs. Greene.'

The irony was lost on her as she ordered Nell to take the candles so that she and Jessie could lift me up and get me back to my bed.

'Shall I get Dr. Stannard?' asked Mrs. Greene when they had struggled gamely through the door and planted me back on my featherbed. 'I could send Tom Greenlaw.'

I winced, holding my ankle and screwing up my face with the pain of it.

'Not at this time of night. Can you put a bandage on it for me? We'll call the doctor to-morrow.'

When the bandage was firmly wound round the aching limb, I felt a little better. Mrs. Greene straightened up from her labours, gently covering me with the sheet.

'What were you doing, Miss Selina? Oh! I see, your carafe is empty. You went to get some water? Jessie, you careless girl. You didn't fill Miss Selina's water-jug to-night, and now see what's happened.'

I let the luckless Jessie take the blame, for I didn't want to tell anyone why I had got up, but I gave her a smile to console her, and after water had been duly procured, together with a glass of hot milk, 'to soothe the nerves' as Mrs. Greene put it, the staff departed and left me alone.

I was considerably shaken, not only by the force with which I had fallen, but with the fact that I was certain I had not merely stumbled over in the dark. It was for all the world as though I had tripped over something stretched across the stairs, although by the time Isa, Mrs. Greene and the others had arrived, and were lugging me manfully up the flight again, there was nothing to be seen. I was back on my fantasies once more. I finished my milk, not entirely satisfied.

What was that noise? Thank heavens Gertrude had heard it too, or I should think that was pure imagination as well. A strange, soft, creaking sound; difficult to locate or identify. Almost as if someone were walking stealthily about the house, but that wasn't possible.

I lay back, putting the matter out of my mind, and much to my surprise fell asleep quite quickly.

The next morning David Stannard arrived, examined my ankle and pronounced a mere strain, fixing a more expertly-wound bandage round it, and advising rest for a few days. That duty done, he sat by my bed and considered me thoughtfully.

'You don't look as blooming as you did when you first arrived, Selina,' he said finally. 'I've been watching you.'

'I'm flattered,' I replied cautiously, 'but I'm quite all right.'

'I think not. You're still brooding about this silly business of Cassie Van Doren's letter to you, aren't you? My dear, there's simply nothing in what she said. It was years ago she wrote, wasn't it, and when you asked her to tell you what bothered her, she didn't reply. Why are you so concerned about it now? Take my advice and forget all about it. Take another piece of advice too.'

'What is that? You look very serious.'

'I am.' He didn't smile. 'I think you should go back to London, at least for a while. This place is getting on your nerves. Your aunt's death was a shock to you and it started you thinking about that old letter. Not only that, you were grieved by Gertrude's departure, weren't you?'

'Yes.' I was honest with David. 'I thought she would never leave me, and I'd no idea she'd even got an aunt living in these parts.'

He sighed. 'No, I understand, but it's not only you who are upset. You are beginning to disturb others too, you know.'

'Oh no! What do you mean?'

I was stricken. Had I been so selfish, and worried my new friends to that extent?

'I was thinking about Oriel Stewart,' he said. 'Chloe has told me that you have been trying to question her, and that she has been hysterical as a result of it.'

I had the grace to look contrite.

'Yes, I did try to ask her some questions. I hadn't meant to upset her so. Has Marcus Tarrant complained to you about me?'

David raised his head.

'Tarrant? No, should he have done?'

'Oriel is his ward. He has complained to me, I can tell you, and in no uncertain terms.'

David smiled slightly.

'Well, there you are. Oriel and her guardian both put out by what you are doing, and we, that is, Anthony, Chloe and I, feel that you are making yourself ill trying to hunt down this imaginary thing from the past. We've grown very fond of you, my dear, although we haven't known you for long. We think you should get away for a while, and forget

122

all about it. Take a holiday; it'll do you good.'

'You're very sweet, and I appreciate your concern for me. I've grown fond of all of you too, but I can't leave here yet, not even for a short while.'

'Why not?'

'Gertrude might write to me again.'

'Letters can be forwarded,' he said quietly. 'Think about it, anyway, and I'll come and see you to-morrow.'

When he had gone, I did feel rather ashamed of myself. It was true enough that in my desire to find out what Cassie had meant, I had rather ignored the feelings of others, and, of course, they knew nothing of my aunt's recent letter and her desperate plea. I had reduced poor Oriel to quivering terror on two occasions; infuriated Tarrant; bored and concerned my new friends with my persistence about what they believed to be mere imagination on my part.

Thus, I was feeling rather low and unsure of what I should do, when Anthony Sewall arrived with a flat parcel under his arm. He was shewn into my bedroom by Jessie, not too shocked at my receiving a male visitor there, since he was, after all, a relation. When she had gone, he bent and kissed me, and it wasn't a cousinly salute. He laughed when

123

he saw my startled expression.

'Serves you right,' he said as he began to open the parcel. 'No woman should have lips as inviting as yours.'

'Anthony! We are cousins.'

'That makes no difference, at least not to me.'

I watched him remove the wrapping, studying the suntanned skin, firm mouth, and vivid blue eyes. Not in Marcus Tarrant's class, of course, but very personable nevertheless.

'What is that?' I asked finally, turning quickly away from the subject of Tarrant. 'Is it a present for me?'

'It is, my lovely.' He grinned. 'Cassie said I couldn't paint and would never be able to do so. What do you think?'

He held out the canvas to me, and I took it with a word of thanks.

I looked at it for a long time before I spoke. My refusal to sit for Anthony had not deterred him, for he had contrived a portrait of me from memory. After what Cassie had said of his abilities, I would have expected a chocolate-box version of my face, which he professed to admire so much.

But it was nothing like that. The dark hair, which I wore swept up to the crown of my head, was faithfully reproduced with careful brush strokes, and the creamy tone of my skin could not be faulted. But somehow Anthony had managed to get into my eyes, and the line of my mouth, all the worries and troubles which had beset me in the last few weeks. This was no flattering compliment; it was a well-executed and very perceptive piece of work.

'Cassie was wrong,' I said at last, and laid the canvas down. 'You can paint.'

'I know.' He had no false modesty. 'I could do better still in more exciting surroundings.'

'Are you complaining about Dower Cottage again?'

'Indeed not. It's nothing to do with that. No, it's this whole place, Leyden, and its surrounding monotony. I want to go to Italy, to France, even to London. I need stimulation.'

He put his head on one side.

'David says you need a holiday.'

'I know.' I grimaced. 'He made it sound as though you, Chloe and he wanted a holiday from me too.'

'Nonsense, no such thing. We are worried about you, and now this fall. Are you in pain?'

'Not very much.'

'Good.' He moved the canvas out of the way and took my hand in his. My fingers looked very white against his sunburnt skin as I felt the slight pressure on them. 'Then as soon as you can walk again, let's go away.'

'Go away? Do you mean . . . '

'I mean you and I. You need a holiday, so your doctor says, and I need inspiration. Let's go to Venice, for there I could paint like the gods.'

'But I don't want to go to Venice, I have to stay here to . . . '

'You don't have to stay here at all. Come to Venice with me. It will do you a world of good, and me too.' The pressure on my hand increased. 'What do you say?'

I didn't want to say anything at that moment, and so I prevaricated, pretending that I would think about it when my ankle was healed. Anthony seemed satisfied enough, and propped my portrait up on the dressing-table.

'There, study yourself, and consider the difference you find in what I saw in you, and what you yourself saw in the mirror before you arrived here. I'll come in again to-morrow.'

I received another kiss, equally disturbing, and lay back to contemplate the painting.

Anthony was gifted; there was no doubt about that. He had looked beyond the flesh and into the soul in the most uncomfortable way. He was also growing rather more affectionate than I cared for, and the remembrance of his lips on mine made me frown.

I hoped that he wasn't getting any wrong ideas about our relationship for, attractive though he was, I could not respond to his overtures. If I ever married, it would not be to a man like Anthony Sewall, but rather to someone like . . .

I broke off, furious with myself. Of course I wouldn't marry Marcus Tarrant, and he certainly would not want me.

I took one last look at my portrait; then I closed my eyes and went to sleep.

6

My ankle did not take long to mend, but during the time I was forced to lie on a sofa, chafing with impatience, I had been making a mental balance sheet of all that had happened since that afternoon in Grey's Hotel, Knightsbridge.

On the assumption that the whole thing was no more than my over-active imagination; one could discount Cassie's letter as that of a senile and sick woman. The jewellery was still missing, despite many searches the staff and I had made, but that did not mean that it was not here in Steeple Court. It simply meant that we had not yet found its hiding place.

As to the rather unpleasant surprise I had when I discovered that Cassie had a waxworks gallery; well, why shouldn't she have had one, if it pleased her? I still found it strange that despite the details which she had given of her life in Leyden, she had never once mentioned the gallery, but perhaps it had never occurred to her that I would be interested.

My new friends and neighbours, to say

nothing of the Romanies, had all assured me time and time again that nothing happened in Leyden years ago. If that was a lie, it was difficult to imagine a conspiracy embracing such a mixed bag of people. Only Oriel Stewart had reacted to my questions, but perhaps I was wrong about her too. Perhaps she did cry readily, and for no good reason, for to all intents and purposes she was a five-year old child.

Maybe I had merely stumbled on the stairs: it could be that my visit to the gallery after dark had filled me with terror, simply because I had expected to experience such an emotion. Since Cassie Van Doren was dead, I couldn't possibly have seen her there, nor could the gipsy boy have turned round by himself.

Gertrude might well have gone off with her aunt, believing it to be her duty. After all, she had left two notes for me; she hadn't simply vanished into thin air without a word. She had been my personal maid, not my possession. She was as free to go south as any bird of the air.

Then I switched my mind to the other side of the ledger. I was certain in my own heart that Cassie had not been senile nor so sick that her communication to me was the mere rambling of a feverish brain. She really had had something she wanted to tell me, and, perhaps conveniently, she was dead before she could speak to me. The jewels had not been found, but perhaps they were not merely hidden, but stolen, and Cassie had not reported the theft because it had something to do with what she feared so much.

That night in the gallery might have produced phantoms of the mind; then again it might not. I was not normally such a nervous person, but there had been a noise; I was sure of that. I was almost certain too, although not quite, that I had seen a figure remarkably like that in the portrait of Cassie.

And Gertrude. This was the hardest thing of all to accept. I could not get it out of my head that there was something wrong about her notes. Why should Gertie write to me when I was so nearby? Why hadn't she come and told me about her aunt, of whom, incredibly, she had never spoken before despite the intimacy of our relationship. I knew without conceit how much she cared for me. Would she really go off and leave me in such a way? And was it not excessively strange that her disappearance had prevented her from telling me whom she had seen in the corridor on the night before she had gone?

But if these peculiarities, which I had tried so hard to thrust into the back of my mind, had any truth in them, what was behind it all? To be more exact, who was behind it all? I let my mind skim over the list of those people now forming my circle, which had once been Cassie's.

Anthony, David, Chloe, Isa Hedley and the servants; the colonel and his wife; the nervous Misses Fanshawe; the vicar, Mr. Blake, and, of course, Marcus Tarrant and his ward. It was extremely difficult to imagine any of them being responsible for the things I had placed on the black side of my ledger.

I was feeling decidedly unhappy, rising from the sofa and walking through the french windows into the garden. I had hardly hobbled a few yards before I saw Marcus Tarrant. He was not in riding habit this time, but dressed with sartorial perfection in morning coat and narrow trousers. I was glad that he was one of the few men of the age who wore neither beard, moustache, nor unbecoming bushy side-whiskers, for they would have ruined the clean, hard planes of his face. I brushed aside my inane thought as he came up to me.

'Well, what have you done with her?'

The riding crop might have gone, but

the clenched fist at his side looked equally dangerous.

I stared at him blankly, noting the unpleasant gleam in his tiger-eyes.

'Done with whom?'

'You know damn well with whom. With Oriel, of course.'

'Oriel?' I must have sounded more vacant than ever, for I had no idea what he was talking about. 'What do you mean, Oriel? Why should she be here?'

'Because you invited her, no doubt, so that you could ignore my warnings and go on tormenting her. Where is she?'

'I have no idea, Sir Marcus. I haven't seen her since that day I visited The Grange.'

'I don't believe you.' His jaw was like carved granite. 'You are the only one who could be responsible. Now answer me! Where is she?'

'I have told you,' I replied acidly, my surprise quickly melting into vexation. 'I have no idea. I haven't seen her. You may not be aware of it, but I have been in bed for the last few days with a strained ankle. I fell downstairs.'

'Really?' He was totally unmoved by my misfortune. 'You should be more careful.'

'I was being careful,' I retorted, 'but my candle had gone out and I had to get downstairs in the dark, and I thought . . . '

He raised one eyebrow.

'Why did you have to go downstairs in the dark, and what did you think?'

'I heard a noise. It was not the first time.' Again I found myself wondering why I was telling Tarrant of my troubles, but somehow it did not seem to stop me. 'Gertie heard the noise too, just before she . . . she left, and I thought . . . No, I'm being stupid.'

'Probably,' he said unchivalrously, 'yet I would still like to know what you thought.'

'I don't think I stumbled.' I was looking down at the grass, not wanting him to see the nervousness in me. 'It was as if I had tripped over something, yet when the servants came and picked me up, there was nothing there.'

'You have a remarkable capacity for making the simplest things a mystery,' he said shortly. 'I'm sorry you were hurt, but that doesn't answer my question. Where is Oriel? If you don't tell me, I shall search Steeple Court, whether you like it or not, and I shall not miss so much as one dark corner of it.'

'Darling, how masterful you are.'

Neither of us had heard Chloe Oldfield approach. She was smiling at us, apricot-coloured chiffon floating behind her, a gay matching parasol over her pretty head.

'Whatever do you want to search Selina's house for? What have you lost, that you think she has stolen from you?'

'Oriel is missing,' he replied tersely. 'She's been gone for a day and a half. She's never before been away as long as that, and Miss Rochford is the only one whom I know who has questioned her until she has been reduced to near dementia. I thought the inquisition might have started again.'

'Oh, Marcus!' Chloe slipped a proprietary arm through his. 'Selina might have asked a few questions, but remember she doesn't understand Oriel as we do. Besides, how could Selina have taken Oriel? Selina has been laid up with a bad ankle, poor love.'

'So I understand, but . . . '

Chloe was soothing.

'Marcus, you're quite wrong about this. Selina wouldn't do such a thing, and David, Anthony and I have been visiting her regularly since the accident. If Oriel had been here, we should have seen her.'

'Then where is she?'

'Probably in the woods.' Chloe's small gloved hand tightened on Marcus's arm, and she was smiling tenderly at him. 'You know how much she likes to go there.'

'Maybe, but why hasn't she come home? She always does, even when she goes to the

134

woods. Besides, we've looked there.'

'Well, perhaps she was hiding and forgot that time was passing. You know how she is. Come, let's go and look for her. Don't worry; I'm sure we shall find her.'

I watched them go with mixed feelings. In one way I was glad that Chloe had arrived, for frankly I had not felt ready for another battle with Tarrant. Yet, perversely, I had not liked the way she had taken his arm, nor the warm intimacy of her smile. It was true that Marcus hadn't responded, but that didn't make me feel any better.

I returned to the house, wondering if Marcus really did love Oriel, not just as his ward, but in another way. Certainly Chloe was deeply in love with Marcus, of that there could be no doubt. Neither idea was palatable, and I found myself thoroughly depressed as I limped back to my sofa and sat down again.

★ ★ ★

The next day I went back to the Romanies. I knew that even if they had any knowledge of Aunt Cassie's secret, they wouldn't tell me about it, but now it was something else which made me seek them out.

It had rained all day, the first time the

perfection of that late June had been spoiled, and so I waited until the drizzle had stopped before I left the grounds of Steeple Court.

I felt rather silly as I approached the encampment. It was well-known that gipsies were fortune-tellers; equally well-known that they duped the gullible by taking their money and repaying them with a lot of nonsense, yet I could not resist the urge to ask the *bibi* about something which was becoming a growing concern to me.

It was still dull and overcast, and the fire looked cheerful as I walked up to the waggons, glistening even more since their wash with the soft summer rain.

There were more of the Romanies present this time, gathering, no doubt, for the evening meal. I saw the *kako* and five younger men; three girls, with red lips, white teeth and long skirts, keeping their legs covered in the way which had met with my aunt's approval. Nevertheless, for all their modesty, their black hair and eyes and glittering trinkets made them extremely attractive as they moved gracefully between the waggons, bringing food to the older women who were cooking in a pot over the fire.

The *bibi* was on the steps where I had last seen her, still smoking her clay pipe. The noisy chatter, in a language wholly foreign to me, stopped at once as I approached, but they were not so suspicious this time, and the *kako* even nodded his head to me.

I bade them all good-evening and offered them the chocolates I had brought for the children. They accepted with grave dignity, ordering the excited youngsters off to eat their sweets away from the adults so we should not be disturbed.

'Well, my deari?' The *bibi* gave me a gummy smile. 'More questions?'

I was embarrassed, but nodded quickly.

'Yes, in a way, but not like those I asked before.'

She eyed me reflectively.

'No? Then what this time, pretty one?'

Still feeling an idiot, I said slowly:

'I'm told that you can tell fortunes. That you can see into the future, and sometimes back into the past.'

'Aye.' The *bibi* was cautious. 'But not about . . .'

'No, no, I told you it wasn't about that. It's something else.'

'What may that be?'

'It's about my maid, Gertrude.'

The *bibi*'s eyes had many wrinkles round them, as if she were very old, but they were as shrewd and sharp as any I had ever seen.

'What about her?'

'She left suddenly. She said she had gone south with her aunt. At least she didn't say it . . . that is . . . she didn't come and tell me about it herself. She wrote two notes, but I'm not sure that she really did write them, nor that she has gone with her aunt.'

The Romanies were very still and quiet, waiting respectfully for the *bibi* to speak, but they seemed to move a bit closer, as if they were interested in what I was saying.

'Why don't you believe it?'

'I'm not sure. I feel foolish, coming to you like this, but I can't rid myself of the idea that something has happened to her. Can you help me? Is there any way that you can tell if all is well with her?'

'Maybe.' The *bibi* put aside her pipe. 'This maid of yours: she's that lanky creature with red hair, isn't she?'

'Yes. Why. Do you know her?'

'We've seen her.' The old woman cackled. 'No question of her running away with a lover, for she's as plain as a plank.'

She must have seen the look on my face, for she beckoned me nearer.

'Let me see your hand.'

'My hand?' I said vaguely, not under-standing her. 'What for? It is Gertrude who is missing . . . that is . . . who has gone.'

'She'll shew up in your hand. You have silver?'

I nodded and passed the money over. Then the *bibi* pushed back the shawl covering her arm, her brown hand knotted with age holding mine as she looked at my palm.

The silence was like a blanket round us. The *bibi* and I could have been alone, for none of the others seemed even to breathe.

After a long time, the *bibi* said quietly:

'She's not here.'

'No, I know. I told you, she's gone.'

She looked up at me, dark, lizard-like eyes gleaming in the light of the fire.

'I do not mean that. She's not in your hand.'

'I don't understand.'

The old woman was patient.

'You were close, you two, weren't you?'

'Yes, very.'

'Then if she were still living I should see her here, no matter where she had gone. But I don't see her. She is no longer alive.'

'No!' I couldn't help the exclamation. 'No, no, it isn't possible. You must be mistaken.'

'I'm never mistaken.' The *bibi* was not offended, appreciating my reluctance to accept her truth. 'Never wrong, Missie. If this woman were alive, I should see her clear as day in your palm. But she's not there. She's dead.'

For a moment our eyes met, and I could see the flicker of compassion in the old woman's. In that fleeting second I recalled something else which I had read in Cassie's notes on the Romanies. She had said that the *bibi* had the special care of the women of the tribe and their problems. She had probably had to deal with grief like mine many times before.

Slowly our hands parted. The *bibi* wrapped the shawl round herself once more and picked up her pipe.

'You should go away from here,' she said finally. 'Your life isn't safe either. There is someone trying to harm you: I saw that too.'

I felt alarm mingle with my sorrow as I looked at her quickly.

'Who?'

'Can't tell you that. You have an enemy. Go away, my deari, while you can. They've got rid of your woman; they'll try for you next.'

'They? But who is it, and is there more than one person?'

'Don't know. Not clear. Just the danger round you is certain. Go while you can.'

She closed her eyes as if she had dropped off into a deep sleep, and I made my faltering *adieux* to the others, limping back to Steeple Court. It was nonsense; of course it was nonsense. How could the old woman be so sure that Gertie was not alive just by looking at my hand?

Yet as I went wearily upstairs to my room, I knew that she was right. It was something which I had sensed from the very first moment Gertie was found to be missing. Absurd though it was to believe in fortune-telling, I agreed with the *bibi*. Gertie hadn't gone south. Gertie was dead.

★ ★ ★

That night as I went to my room and began to undress, my heart was like a leaden lump in my breast. Although most people would have ridiculed me for believing the old woman, I had really known from the beginning that Gertie had not simply walked off and left me. I had tried to pretend to myself that the two notes, alleged to have been written by her, were genuine, and that she really did have an aunt with whom she had gone away, but I had never been entirely convinced. Now I had to face a dreadful truth, even though it was based on the words of a Romany fortune-teller and my own instincts.

And that was not all. If I believed what the *bibi* had said about Gertie, I ought to begin to wonder whether what she had said of me was also true. Was I in danger? If so, from whom? All the nasty little things on my mental balance sheet came flooding back to me, and as I let my petticoat slip to the floor I felt suddenly cold.

It must have something to do with Cassie's letter, and what she had told me of her secret. And did that secret involve the missing jewellery which was said to be so valuable? If anyone was trying to do me a mischief, that might be the motive. A fortune in gems, which no one could find.

The shudder passed off, and then I felt hot, stifled in the confines of my room, elegant though it was. I opened the bottom of the window as wide as I could, watching the rose-garden for a minute or two by the light of the moon.

Then I went to the dressing table and took the pins out of my hair, letting the dark tresses fall down my back. I studied my face very carefully in the mirror. Anthony, with his artist's eye, had been right, and honest. I had changed. It was difficult to see exactly how, for my skin was milk-white as before, yet perhaps there was a little less colour in the cheeks. And had there been that worried crease between my eyebrows before I came here, and those tiny lines, almost imperceptible, at each corner of my mouth?

But it was really the eyes which told the truth. They were no longer bright and carefree. They were large and dark, as before, fringed with long lashes, but there was something in them which Anthony had seen first, and which I could see now. It wasn't pleasant.

When I had brushed my hair, I stood and looked at myself in the full-length mirror, unashamed of my body which, I consoled myself, was every bit as good as Oriel Stewart's.

I turned off the gasolier and then blew out the candle, making do with the moonlight as I reached for my nightgown. Then I heard the sound at the window and looked round quickly.

I could feel the chill again as I saw the outline of a man, and groped frantically for my robe. He poised himself on the sill for a second or two, but before I could cover my nakedness he was across the room.

We struggled silently for a full minute. I had no idea who he was, for he had something over his face, only his eyes gleaming through the slits in the cloth. He was strong; I was sure of that, if of nothing else. My puny efforts to hold him off were useless, and I found myself thrown to the floor with such a force that it knocked the breath out of me.

My fears were purely of rape. I thought the stranger had come to take me, for it would have been easy enough for him to have climbed up the wall round the rose-garden, which was rough, with plenty of footholds and ivy to give him a hand. He could have been watching me as I had undressed and looked at myself in the glass, and I went hot with shame and fear.

Thus, when I felt the whip cut across my shoulders I gasped not only with pain but in startled disbelief, for that was the last thing I had expected. When I cried out at the second blow, a pillow was thrust over my head to stifle my voice.

Naturally I fought, turning and twisting to try to escape the savage attack, but the man was too strong for me. He appeared to be holding the suffocating pillow down with one foot, whilst he wielded the lash without mercy.

I have no idea how long my punishment went on. It seemed as though it was never going to stop, and beneath the muffling feathers I was sobbing in pain.

Finally he was done, at least with the whip,

but when he hauled me up, it was not to release me but to impart his last spurt of venom. I felt his fist on my eye and cheek and then meet my jaw with a force which hurled me backwards to the floor again. After that, I remembered nothing more until I came to some minutes later.

I dragged myself up, unable to believe what had happened, wondering why none of my household had come to help me. But, of course, there had been no noise, apart from my one cry. The whole thing had been almost silent from the moment I had first seen the intruder on the sill. At last I got to the window to close it, fastening the catch with unsteady fingers.

When I staggered over to the mirror, I almost screamed aloud. I was a terrible sight, with blood on my face and dark bruises beginning to form round my eye and on my cheek. And as for my body! With great difficulty I twisted round, seeing the weals which the beating had caused, whimpering as I collapsed on the bed and began to shake helplessly.

After a while I stopped. It was no good lying there in that state, and I managed to pour water from the jug on the washstand into the painted china basin, to bathe the worst of the damage.

When I was safely clad in my nightgown and wrap, the shock at last beginning to lessen, I remembered the *bibi*'s words. Is that what she had meant? An enemy, who wished to harm me. My mouth twisted. Certainly he'd done that, whoever he was.

On the assumption that it was not a passing tramp, nor a maniac, who could have done this to me and why? The answer was not so hard to find, and fresh tears sprang into my eyes.

The only man who was capable of this brutality, at least to my knowledge, was Marcus Tarrant, and he had threatened me more than once. I supposed that he and Chloe had not found Oriel in the woods, and so he had kept his promise. He had warned me he would not use words again, and he hadn't.

I buried my hands in my face and began to cry in earnest, and it was not because of the shame or pain, but for some quite different reason.

When I had finished with my grief, I wondered whether to call Mrs. Greene or Jessie. Then I decided against it. Certainly they would believe that I had been attacked, for the proof was obvious enough, but I didn't want to have to tell them whom I believed was responsible.

I took a sleeping draught and got into bed, sore in body and mind. To-morrow, if I could get myself up, I would go and see Marcus Tarrant. No one was going to treat me like this and remain immune from retribution.

I hadn't taken his precious ward, and I was damned if I was going to be molested for something of which I was entirely innocent. I turned gingerly on my side and closed my eyes, furious with myself because I could feel the last few tears squeeze under my lids and roll down my cheeks.

7

I pretended I was still sleepy when Jessie brought my tea and pulled back the curtains, keeping the bedclothes well over me until she had gone, just murmuring that I should not want breakfast that morning.

I drank the tea before I tried to get out of bed, and found that I ached in every limb as I made for the mirror. My face was less battered than I had feared. My lip had shrunk to normal size, my cheek no longer bleeding. When I had washed, I sat down with my pots of cream, rouge and powder and began to cover up what I could of the ugly marks.

I managed to get out of the house about eleven o'clock without anyone seeing me. I spotted the Mouse on the stairs, making her way to the gallery, but mercifully her thoughts must have been on her charges for she did not look over the banisters.

I didn't call for my carriage either, for Tom Greenlaw, though not a particularly intelligent man, could not fail to see that something was amiss with me. Somehow I managed to get to The Grange on foot. It took time, and once or twice I almost fell in the long grass and on the uneven ground.

When I was shewn into Tarrant's library, he rose from his chair, eyebrows elevated in anything but a welcome.

'Yes? What is it?' He was as blunt and discourteous as usual. 'Have you come to tell me what you've done with Oriel?'

'No, I haven't, for the simple reason that I have not seen her, as I told you. Does that mean you have not found her yet?'

'It does.' The curt words did not quite conceal his worry. 'Then if you have not come to confess, what have you come for?'

I moved towards the desk, and suddenly his eyes narrowed.

'Your face. What's the matter with it? You look like a painted harlot.'

'No doubt I do,' I snapped back, 'but I didn't want anyone to see the bruises you inflicted on me last night.'

'What the devil are you talking about?' He came round the desk and tilted my chin, his mouth hardening as he could see at close quarters the reason for my mask of rouge and powder. 'Good God; who did this?'

'I assumed it was you.' I jerked my face away from his hand. 'It was you who said you would not use words next time, and you didn't, did you?'

'Will you talk sense!'

He was sharp, catching me by the shoulders so that I cried out in pain. He let me go as if I had scalded his fingers.

'What is it? I hardly touched you.'

'This morning, no, but last night you were somewhat less gentle.' I could hear my voice quavering, exasperated because I couldn't control myself. 'Last night you used that damned whip of yours, didn't you?'

For a moment Marcus remained silent. Then he said very softly:

'Are you trying to tell me that someone attacked you last night?'

'I am, and don't pretend that . . .'

'You say with a whip?'

'Yes, and you're very fond of carrying one.'

'But not for the purpose of beating women, however aggravating they may be. Stop being such a fool. I didn't do this. Surely you could see who the man was.'

'No . . . no. I'd put out the lights, and he had something over his face, but I assumed it was you, because . . .'

'My dear Miss Rochford.' His voice was languid now. 'If ever I should decide to teach you a lesson, I would make no secret of it, believe me. Now, since I did not lay a finger on you, who else would do such a thing? Whom, apart from me and my ward, have you been upsetting?'

I was very nearly in tears again, and he must have have seen it, for his voice grew a trifle less grating.

'Could it have been those gipsies? I warned you not to go near them again. Did you do so?'

'Yes . . . yes I did, but to ask them different questions this time. You'll think me mad if I tell you.'

'I think you're mad now,' he replied uncharitably, 'so you might as well confirm my worst suspicions. Why did you go back to them, knowing that they couldn't, or wouldn't, tell you anything?'

'I went to see if . . . if . . . the . . . the old woman could . . . could . . . '

'Could what?' He was vastly impatient. 'Stop stammering, girl. See if the old woman could do what?'

I got out my handkerchief, for I had a feeling that I was going to need it before long.

'I wanted to know if she could see into the future, or back into the past.'

'For heaven's sake!'

I went on, ignoring his scorn.

'And whether she could tell me what had happened to Gertie.'

The expression on his face changed; the irritation was gone, and something watchful had taken its place.

'I see. And what did she have to say when you had crossed her palm with silver?'

'You'll only scoff if I tell you.'

'I'm past scoffing. What did she say?'

I gave a deep sigh and wiped the corners of my eyes, no longer caring whether he saw my tears or not.

'She said she couldn't see Gertie in my hand any more. That if she were alive, no matter where she was, she would have seen her. She is dead, according to the *bibi*.'

'The *bibi*?'

'The old woman. *Bibi* means auntie. She's really the one who controls the family, although there is a nominal leader; the eldest male.'

'You seem to know a good deal about these gipsies,' he said grimly, 'but I could have told you that the tale about your maid's departure was probably untrue, and you would not have needed to cross my palm with silver.'

'Why are you so sure?' I looked up at him, the sight of his face and odd-coloured eyes making my pulse race. 'How can you know?'

'It seems obvious to me.' He was off-hand.

'But since you think me capable of breaking into Steeple Court in the middle of the night and giving you a flogging, which I am bound to say I think you richly deserved, perhaps I did away with your maid too. A possibility, don't you think?'

I rose to my feet with some difficulty, for I was growing stiffer than ever.

'The only thing I think is that you are both rude and cruel. I assumed that you were responsible for what had happened last night, but now I think I was wrong. As you say, had you done such a thing, you would have boasted about it.'

'You have a very low opinion of me, Miss Rochford.'

There was a faint smile on his lips.

'It is about as low as your opinion of me, Sir Marcus. Good-day.'

Suddenly his levity was gone.

'You'd better see Stannard.'

'Why? To ask him if he was responsible? I can assure you that David would not do such a thing.'

'You can't be sure about anybody, but that was not what I meant. You need treatment, and Stannard is a doctor.'

'I can manage without treatment. Now, if you will ring for your . . . '

Before either of us could say another word,

the french windows opened and there was Oriel Stewart. She looked like a fresh spring morning, in her long green dress and silver-gold hair loose about her shoulders. She smiled at Marcus, her eyes alight as she moved towards him.

I expected him to berate her for frightening him with her long absence from home, but it appeared that he kept his bad temper for me.

'Oriel.' He put his arm round her, pulling her to him as he kissed her cheek. 'I've missed you, love, where have you been?'

I felt the pang I was begining to grow used to as I saw the way Marcus held Oriel against him, and watched him as he looked down at her.

'I've been in the garden.' She nestled closer to him. 'I was only in the garden, Marcus. Why didn't you call if you wanted me?'

I met Marcus's eyes for a single second. They contained a warning which could not be misunderstood. Oriel was not to know that she had been missing for two days, and I was not to open my interfering mouth and tell the silly girl that her guardian had been frantic for her safety for the last forty-eight hours. I wondered in that moment where she had actually been. Not in the woods, apparently, for Marcus and Chloe had looked there, but, of course, there were plenty of other places where she might have hidden herself, oblivious to the passing of the hours.

Then Marcus rang for his butler and I was shewn to the door, but not before I cast a backward look at him, seeing him bend his head once more to kiss Oriel's forehead.

I felt sick at heart and entirely alone when the butler had closed the door behind me, as slowly and painfully I began to make my way back to Steeple Court.

★ ★ ★

Since I was now convinced that Tarrant was not responsible for attacking me, there was no reason to keep the matter to myself any longer. Mrs. Greene and Jessie put soothing ointment on my back, horrified by what they saw, and fearful that something similar might happen again, perhaps this time to them.

'It was those tinkers.' Jessie's face was white. 'That's who it was, Miss Selina. They're a rough lot, and perhaps they didn't like you going to their camp. Shall we send Tom to Little Horton. There's a policeman there.'

'No, no.' I brushed the idea aside at once. 'I'm all right now, and I'm sure there will be no repetition of this.'

'But I'm going to lock my windows to-night just the same.' Jessie was quite unconvinced by my assurance. 'You do the same, Miss Selina, or next time they might kill you.'

I had washed off my rouge and powder, so that when Chloe called on me later that day she let out a small shriek.

'Selina! What on earth has happened? What have you done to your face? Darling, you have a black eye and . . . '

'Yes, yes, I know.' I shepherded her to a chair and rang for coffee. 'And that's not all.'

'What do you mean?'

She was concerned for me, holding my hand, yet eager to hear more of my misfortune. When I told her she paled.

'I should have died if it had happened to me,' she said at last. 'How brave you are. Have you called David?'

'No, nor am I going to do so. I'm quite all right now. It's over and done with, and I don't want a fuss made.'

'But who did it?'

I shrugged.

'I've told you, I don't know. It was dark, and the man's face was covered. He was very strong though. I thought it was Marcus Tarrant and went to accuse him of it, but it was clear that he knew nothing about it.'

'Marcus!' Chloe gasped. 'Why on earth should he . . . oh yes . . . I see. Because of Oriel.'

'Who has now returned home, by the way.'

'Has she indeed? And where was she?'

'She says in the garden.'

'For two days?'

'So she insists.'

'Of course, she's quite insane. Was Marcus angry with her?'

I waited until Jessie had poured the coffee and left the room before I replied.

'Not in the least. He embraced her and kissed her most affectionately. I don't think anything Oriel does makes him angry.'

'No.' Chloe looked almost old. 'You're right, of course, nothing does. There's a rumour going about, you know, that he may marry her, so that she has the protection of his name.'

I felt as if my stomach had done a somersault, but my hand was steady on the coffee cup.

'Really? I should have thought he was protective enough already.'

'So would I, but that's what's being said. Oh, Selina, it's such a waste! What can she do for him? What can she possibly give him?'

'Her beauty.' I said it without expression. 'She's very lovely, and perhaps Marcus doesn't like intelligent women. Some men have a need to protect the helpless. Maybe he is such a man.'

Chloe hardly seemed to have heard me.

'If he marries her, I shall die, I know I shall. I love him so much, yet although he dines with me now and then, and would probably say I was his friend, were he asked, I sometimes wonder if he is even aware of my existence.'

'I'm sure he is.' I had to try to comfort Chloe, although I knew it was wrong to foster hope when there was no hope to be had. 'He probably feels responsible for the girl, and she is a dear, despite the fact that she is . . . '

'Mad?' Chloe's laugh was as hard as tempered steel. 'Mad is the word, Selina, and I wonder how Marcus will enjoy making love to a lunatic.'

Even that jar to my heart did not weaken my fingers round the handle of the cup. I didn't want to think of things like that, but Chloe was forcing me to do so.

'I expect the rumours are wrong,' I said, when my voice was under control again. 'Surely Tarrant will want an heir. He wouldn't chance that heir being . . . well . . . '

Chloe gave a sudden wide smile.

'Thank God for your common sense, Selina. What would I do without it? Yes, of course, Marcus will need a son, but not one tainted with his mother's insanity, so perhaps there is a chance for me yet. Who knows?'

★ ★ ★

When Chloe had gone, I went up to the gallery and found the Mouse hard at work on the hem of Marie-Antoinette's gown. She looked up, a vexed frown on her face.

'There's a big tear here, Miss Rochford,' she said testify, 'I can't think how it has happened, for I'm always so careful, and no one ever comes up here but you and me. I suppose you didn't . . . '

'No, not I.' I was thinking back to that awful night in the gallery when I could so easily have ripped the lace flounce in my panic. 'Never mind, I'm sure you'll be able to repair it.'

'Oh yes, it's not that it's difficult, but I don't like these things to happen.'

'Miss Hedley, that gipsy boy.'

'Yes?' The Mouse kept her head bent, intent on her needle. 'What about him?'

'Does he always stand round that way, or do you move him sometimes?'

'Move him?' Then Isa's head did shoot up, shocked as if I had accused her of breaking the figure into a thousand pieces. 'Oh no, Miss Rochford, I would never move anything. Miss Van Doren always chose the position and way in which the figures were to stand, and I wouldn't dream of altering them. Of course, if you wanted . . . '

'No, no, I just wondered. I thought when I was up here not long ago he was facing the other way, but I must have been mistaken.'

The Mouse's anxiety faded, and she gave a small titter.

'Not difficult to imagine things going on up here, is it? I was told that Mr. Anthony and Miss Chloe wagered you would not spend fifteen minutes in the gallery at midnight. Were you frightened?'

'Not really,' I lied shamelessly. 'It was rather dark, of course, and my candle was making queer shapes on the wall, which didn't help, but I stayed the course, and won the bet.'

'And you didn't see anything?' Isa was sly. 'Nothing out of the way?'

'Only Henry VIII waltzing with Anne Boleyn.' I was cool, for I didn't like the look on the Mouse's face. 'Otherwise all seemed well. Perhaps I ought to wager you to do the same thing, Miss Hedley.'

160

I watched the colour drain out of her face, feeling heartless for scaring her, even though a moment ago she had seemed to be laughing at me for what she knew to be my pretence.

'Oh no! I couldn't, I couldn't!' She rose to her feet, her mending finished. 'I love them all, of course, but it isn't the same here after dark. Now, if you'll excuse me, I must see to some things in the workroom.'

I was thoughtful as I went downstairs, pausing in my bedroom to put a light covering of powder over my face in case I should have other visitors. As I touched my cheek with the puff something occurred to me. Isa Hedley had not said: 'It wouldn't be the same thing after dark.' What she had said was: 'It isn't the same thing.' So, she had been in the gallery at night, for all her professed fears.

I forgot about the incident, and when I got to the sitting-room I found Anthony waiting for me.

'Anthony, I didn't know you were here. Jessie should have told me.'

'I asked her not to disturb you. I knew you'd turn up eventually.'

He had risen, but this time all I got was a brief peck on the cheek, and his manner was considerably more subdued than usual.

161

Furthermore, he made no comment about my somewhat battered appearance, which I thought a trifle odd. It was as if he were so preoccupied with his thoughts that he wasn't really seeing me at all.

'It's rather late for tea,' I said as I sat down. 'Would you like whisky? It's over there.'

'There is nothing that I would like more, and a large one at that.'

There was something wrong; I could hear it in his voice, and Anthony was not normally a heavy drinker.

When he was sitting opposite me, he gave a diffident smile.

'I don't quite know how to begin this conversation.'

'Is it so difficult then?' I kept my own voice untroubled, hoping he wasn't going to start talking about Venice again. 'Is something worrying you?'

'I'm afraid it is, and you're the very last person I want to burden with my problems, but there's no one else I know who is in a position to help me.'

I thought about that for a while; then I said even more casually:

'By that, I take it we are discussing the question of money.'

'Shrewd as well as beautiful.' He drained

162

his glass. 'May I have another?'

'Of course. As many as you want.'

'Two will suffice, for I must keep a clear head.'

'Am I so formidable?'

'No, but when one has to ask a woman for help of this kind, it is as well to do it whilst one is fairly sober. Two will give me Dutch courage; three might unman me.'

I was sorry for Anthony, but knowing that embarrassment was the most catching of all diseases I became strictly practical.

'To coin your own phrase, dear coz, are you in need of money? If so, say so, and don't beat about the bush.'

'You make it sound easier than it is.'

'Money is always easy to talk about.'

'Only if you have plenty, and you have always had plenty, Selina, haven't you, even before Cassie left you her fortune?'

If I had blushed or shewn signs of shame because of my wealth, it wouldn't have helped Anthony, so I said briskly:

'Yes, I have. An accident of birth, of course, and no credit to me.'

'Perhaps not, yet you're rich.'

'All right. So I'm rich and nice; shrewd and beautiful, according to you. What next?'

He laughed reluctantly.

'Dearest Selina, how hard you are working

163

to make it simple for me, aren't you. Yes, you're all of those things, and kind too. I wish . . . '

'What?'

'It's nothing. By the way, are you better?' He seemed to see me properly for the first time, frowning as he studied my face. 'I met Chloe just now, and she told me some swine had attacked you. If I knew who it was, I would kill him.'

I brushed his anger aside.

'I'm perfectly all right, so there is no need for me to call upon you for any knight-errantry. Now, about this money. I assume that you have debts.'

He was rather pale, looking down into his half-empty glass.

'Quite a few, I'm afraid.'

'How much will it take to clear them?'

'Not less than two thousand pounds.'

I was shaken. What on earth could Anthony have done in Leyden to amass debts of that kind? He saw my look and shrugged.

'I gamble when I go to York, and that's the truth of it. I've lost a lot over the last six months, and now those to whom I owe the money are becoming somewhat ugly.'

'I see. Very foolish of you, Anthony, but I won't lecture you.' My smile was comforting. 'I'll give you a cheque before you leave.

You'll need more than two thousand if you are to go on eating and buying paints and brushes.'

'You're very generous.' His voice was low. 'I hated to ask, but neither David nor Chloe could give me that sort of assistance.'

'And I'm more than happy to do so. I've always felt that you should have had some of Cassie's money. I shall give you five thousand, and will feel much happier when I have done so.'

'I don't need that much,' he said hastily. 'An extra hundred, perhaps, but . . .'

'Five thousand,' I said firmly. 'Remember, I have to live with myself.'

'I'm more grateful than you will ever know, but it makes it difficult to ask the next question.'

'Oh? What's that?'

'Have you thought any more about Venice?'

I looked at Anthony for a long minute. He was normally good-tempered, merry, easy to look at, and very gifted. It was also obvious that his affection for me was growing into something more than cousinly love. Would I be wise to forget all about a liaison which could never be, and take Anthony to Venice, where he could paint, and where our relationship could grow and blossom?

Then I thought of Marcus Tarrant's face, with its marvellous bones and bright amber eyes. Always offensive, mostly angry, and clearly with no time for me, whom he regarded as a nuisance and a half-wit.

I said gently:

'No, not really. I've not made a final decision, of course. It needs a lot of thinking about.'

'Yes, of course.' He smiled in the old way, his discomfiture over the money forgotten. 'But I can wait. Think about it by all means, and while you're doing that, I shall pray for an affirmative answer.'

'Oriel is back.' I changed the subject. 'She says she was only in the garden, but of course she wasn't, for the grounds were thoroughly searched and so were the fields and woods. Where do you think she went?'

'The Lord alone knows.' Anthony finished his whisky. 'She's such an odd girl, she might have gone anywhere. In a way, I envy her, for nothing seems to touch her. Locked up as she is in her own world, the hardships we have to face don't exist for her.'

'No, Marcus Tarrant sees to that.'

Anthony looked at me curiously.

'You said that with some feeling, my love. Do you find him attractive?'

I was extremely cautious.

166

'It depends what you mean by attractive. If you mean do I think him handsome, like that Ming vase in the corner, well yes, I do. But if you are asking me whether I like him, the answer is no. I find him uncivil and overbearing.'

'Some women like that.' Anthony was teasing me again, quite his old self. 'I'm told they don't mind a man capable of mastering them, and even beating the hell out of them when they deserve it.'

'Beating them?'

'Oh no, I'm not suggesting Tarrant attacked you. He's just a little too civilized for that, but you know what I mean.'

'Yes, I suppose so. Chloe says Tarrant may marry Oriel. Do you think he will?'

'Not if he's got any sense. Pity Chloe's so besotted by Marcus. I don't think he even likes her.'

'Why do you say that?'

'It's just an impression I get. Perhaps I'm wrong.'

'I hope so, for Chloe's sake. Anthony.'

'Mm?'

'Why don't you ever visit the gallery upstairs now? The Mouse says you haven't been there for years.'

'Cassie didn't want me at the house, but in any event I've no feeling for those effigies of hers. Stiff and lifeless. That's not art.'

'But you haven't seen the gipsy boy, the last figure Cassie dressed. He's superb. Do you want to see him?'

'Not particularly.' My cousin was very frank. 'To me, he would look just like the rest of them. I'd rather look at you.'

'Then in that case, I shall write your cheque and you can go home. I'm not in the mood to be looked at to-day.'

'You're a hard woman.'

'But a sensible one. I don't rush into things.'

He took the cheque with another word of thanks, and a far more lingering kiss than before. Then he said quietly:

'Have you made a new Will yet, Selina?'

I was startled.

'A new Will? No, why should I?'

'Because of your legacy from Cassie. Get old Carbury to do it for you. If anything happens to you, you would want your possessions to go to the right people, wouldn't you?'

'Yes . . . yes, I suppose so, but I hate thinking about Wills.'

'Ninny!' He put one arm round me. 'You'll outlive us all, but consider it. It's a sensible thing to do.'

When he had gone, I stood by the bureau

and did as Anthony had suggested. I did think about a new Will and to whom I would want to leave my money. It was only after I had drafted a letter to Cecil Carbury that I wondered why Anthony thought something might befall me.

Then I shook myself. I was being morbid. Everyone had to die sooner or later; sometimes sooner, as in the case of illness. Anthony was merely being practical, and I was being ridiculous, so I began to make a list of small bequests. This done, I stopped, pen poised in mid-air.

But who was going to get Steeple Court and my fortune, to say nothing of the missing jewels? I laid the pen down again. This would need thinking about, and I was glad to find that it was nearly time to dress for dinner. I made for my room, and put the rather uncomfortable subject of my demise out of my head for the moment. To-morrow would be soon enough to consider a new Will.

8

Every so often, between worrying about other things, I would poke into odd corners, tucked-away bureaux and tallboys, to see if I could find the missing gems. Since so many people had already searched with great thoroughness, I did not really expect to meet with success, and was beginning to doubt whether they were at Steeple Court after all.

One morning, when I had nothing better to do, I was looking in a large wardrobe in the dressing-room where Gertrude had slept. I didn't like going there very much, for by now I was certain that the *bibi* was right. Gertie was dead, though why, how, and what had happened, I had no idea, and without some kind of evidence I could hardly approach the police.

My aunt's clothes were still in the wardrobe: mostly rather old-fashioned evening gowns and wraps which she had not used for a long time. I was about to close the door, when I noticed two small drawers right at the back of the cupboard. I felt a sudden quickening of my heart-beat. Had I really found somewhere which everyone else had missed? But I was doomed to disappointment. The first drawer contained a number of fans, the second a musical box.

I took the latter back to my bedroom and tried to make it produce a tune, but it merely uttered a squeak or two and then gave up the effort. Determined not to be outdone by the prettily-painted toy, I turned it over and opened the base. It was no wonder that it was incapable of playing its customary air, for stuffed inside it was a folded paper, jamming its delicate works.

Slowly I unfolded the note, not sure that I wanted to know its contents. Something warned me that I would regret it, for if it were something of no consequence, why had my aunt, or someone else, taken so much trouble to hide it?

It was, in fact, in Cassie's hand, and frankly I could not understand a word of it at my first reading. It began without preamble, nor was it addressed to anyone in particular.

It simply said: 'Look to the heights for that which is precious and beautiful, and to the depths for that which is ugly and evil. For the rest, ask Henry.'

Henry? Who was Henry? I quickly ran over the names of those in Leyden and the nearby houses occupied by the gentry, but came up with nothing. There was no one called Henry to my knowledge. Perhaps it had been the christian name of the deceased Mr. Porter; if so, it was too late to ask him anything.

'Look to the heights.' What had Cassie meant by that? Was she referring to a mountain, or some high part of the Moors? Or had she simply meant the highest place in Steeple Court? I caught my breath.

The gallery was the highest place here, for it was a full flight of stairs above the servants' quarters, on the other side of the house. And the depths? If Cassie had been referring to Steeple Court, and by now I was beginning to think she was, then the lowest place was the basement; the cellars which ran right under the house and its outbuildings. That still did not explain Henry, but I wasted no more time, and put the note into my bureau drawer.

I had seen the Mouse go out about half an hour ago, hoping that she had not returned as I hastened up to the gallery. She hadn't, and I was alone with the rigid figures, endeavouring to fathom out what Cassie had been trying to say.

It occurred to me also that since she had written this message so strangely, she really must have been afraid of something or someone. It was couched in terms designed to confuse and why, if she were not frightened, did she wish to do that?

'That which is beautiful.' I walked slowly amongst the figures. I suppose they were all beautiful in their way, even the villains in their cell. Anthony hadn't thought so, of course, but he saw beauty differently. To him, waxworks were just inanimate objects, not works of art.

Beautiful? The most beautiful to me was the gipsy boy, but that was because something about him fascinated me. Others might find greater loveliness in Marie-Antoinette's tinted cheeks and fabulous gown.

I went to the dais where the royalty stood. Arrogant Henry; the witch Anne Boleyn; Mary Queen of Scots, misleadingly demure in her distinctive headdress, and the unsmiling hero of Agincourt. I turned away, stepping down from the shallow platform, but as I did so I knocked against the Virgin Queen, almost toppling her from her stand. It felt uncanny to hold her stiff body in my arms as I steadied her. Lèse-majesté to say the least of it.

Then I saw that in my carelessness I had dislodged one of the jewels from her gown. It was a large green stone, and it gleamed very brightly in the sunlight.

It was several seconds before I bent to pick it up, because what I was thinking could not possibly be true. It couldn't be that simple. But it was. The emerald was not paste. I knew quite a lot about precious stones, for I had a good few of my own, and my father had been something of an expert too.

I rose to my feet and had a closer look at Elizabeth's gown. Many of the jewels which adorned it were coloured glass, but at least six or seven were not. It was the same with the others: Mary, the French Queen, and the two Henries.

So this was where Cassie had hidden her jewels, but how had she managed to do so without alerting Isa? So few others came up to the gallery that there was hardly any risk that they would notice some genuine stones amongst the welter of paste, but had Cassie really fooled the Mouse?

I thought I heard a sound from the workroom. Perhaps Isa had returned after all, and I slipped the emerald into my pocket and went to find out. There was no one there, and so I took the opportunity of running my fingers through the large box of coloured baubles on the bench. As far as I could tell, not one of them was genuine. If Cassie had chosen a time when Isa Hedley was out, or even in bed, it would not have been difficult for her to have deceived the Mouse, if the latter had no knowledge of gems, and couldn't tell paste from the real thing.

I went back to my room again, holding the emerald up to the light and then putting it into my jewel-case. I noticed that I had left the door open, and closed it quickly. This was the kind of house where anyone could creep along its carpeted corridors and spy, without the object of their interest being aware of it.

And I didn't intend to tell anyone about my find, at least not for the moment. If Cassie had gone to so much trouble to hide her jewels, it was another clear indication that she did not trust those about her, or at least one of those near at hand. I should have to tell Carbury sooner or later, but it could wait for a while.

The next thing to consider were the depths, which, according to Cassie, had something in them which was ugly and evil. So down into the depths I must go. It would have been very difficult for me to get into the cellars without arousing the servants' curiosity if the only access to them had been through the kitchens and other rooms below stairs. Fortunately, however, in my exploration of Steeple Court, in the early days following my arrival, I had discovered a small external door which also led down to the stores.

The cellars were spacious, separated by narrow passages. Some contained coal, others wood. There were smaller rooms crammed with old furniture, cases and boxes etc., and a large wine cellar full of racks with bottles draped in cobwebs.

Only one door was locked. It was at the end of a passage, and although I tried to shift the padlock, I could make no impression on it, as if the room were determined to stay shut against my inquisitive eyes.

I could see nothing there which was evil, or particularly ugly for that matter. They were normal cellars, containing ordinary household things.

What other depths could there be? As I reached the garden again I remembered the disused well, not far from the house. That would have depth: was that what Cassie had meant? I went to look at it. The heavy wooden cover was half-off, so that I was able to squint down, but all I could see was blackness. I threw a pebble into the well, and it was a long time before I heard the slight splash of water. If it were the well to which Cassie had referred, I should have a hard time finding out what was down there.

Back in the house I met Isa. She looked

more tense than ever, and would have rushed off, had I not stopped her.

'I have been to the gallery,' I said cheerfully. 'How well you keep it. I am truly grateful for all your care. Have you been up there this morning?'

Isa shot me a furtive look, her fingers busy twiddling with a jet necklace she wore round her thin throat.

'Not yet, Miss Rochford. I was just on my way. Is there anything you want?'

'No, no, I just wondered. What are you going to do to-day?'

'Well, just the usual cleaning, and then I may start on a new lace collar for Mary Queen of Scots. I noticed that hers was getting rather grimy and worn.'

'Don't forget to dust my gipsy boy,' I said, watching her unsteady lips. 'Don't let anything happen to him, will you?'

She shook her head, her face more pinched than ever.

'No, of course not. Is that all?'

'Thank you, yes.'

She shot off like a startled hare released from a trap, and as I watched her rapid departure I had the distinct feeling that she had been lying. Why should she say she hadn't been up in the gallery that morning, if in fact she had? She was entitled to go

177

there at any time, so why pretend? I gave up, and went back to my room, shutting the door firmly behind me before taking the emerald out of the jewel-case to examine it more closely.

It was magnificent, and worth a fortune in itself. These gems might hold the answer to Cassie's mystery, for they would be worth fighting for. Even worth killing for. Suddenly I felt cold, and shut the stone away quickly.

No one knew where they were, so how could anyone kill for them. I was being neurotic again. Aunt Cassie had died of a heart attack, and the only other person who was dead, or so I believed, was Gertie. It made no sense, yet something rather horrible was going on here, of that I was sure.

★ ★ ★

When I saw Oriel Stewart in my garden the next afternoon, I smiled and waved to her. She came dancing up immediately, even kissing my cheek as if she were pleased to see me.

I thought for a second about Marcus Tarrant, but then I dismissed him from my mind. In this exquisite, witless creature by my side, lay the answer I was looking for. I don't know why I was so sure, but every fibre of my body told me that I was right.

I said gaily:

'How nice to see you, Oriel. Have you come to visit me?'

'Yes, I have. May I have some more chocolate?'

I laughed.

'Of course you may. Come into the house and I'll get you some.'

When she was happily sucking her chocolate bar, I said slowly:

'Oriel, have you ever seen the waxworks gallery which my aunt made at the top of the house?'

'Waxworks?'

There was a frown marring the smooth white brow.

'Yes, waxworks. Don't you know what they are?'

'No, what are they?'

'Figures, made of wood mostly, with wax heads, faces and hands, and dressed up in clothes to shew who they are. They really are rather fine; would you like to see them?'

She nodded, and went on devouring her chocolate.

We met no one on our way up, and fortunately Isa wasn't in the gallery. Gently I detached the sticky bar from Oriel's hand lest the costumes should become soiled if she touched one of them. She didn't mind her loss, for she was immediately entranced by what she saw, crying out in amazement.

She spent a long time looking at the royal figures, cooing with satisfaction at the expensive materials and glittering gems. Certainly Oriel wouldn't recognize which of the latter were genuine and which were not, so I let her examine the costumes as closely as she wished.

'They are like real people,' she said finally. 'Aren't they beautiful. Who is that one?'

'That's Queen Elizabeth, the daughter of Henry VIII, this king over here, and that's Henry V.'

Oriel ignored the martial Henry, and touched the hem of Marie-Antoinette's skirt. I prayed that she would leave no telltale marks for the Mouse to find, but I did not stop her. Her face was wrapt, all her attention on the fine lace-work and silver braid.'

'Marie-Antoinette,' I said after a while. 'She's splendid, isn't she?' I thought it wise not to mention the queen's fate lest it spoiled Oriel's pleasure. 'Let's have a look at some of the others, shall we?'

She pulled a face at the criminals in Newgate, drawing closer to me as if they frightened her.

'Don't worry.' I patted her hand. 'They're

180

only wax models, you know. They can't move, so they can't hurt you either.'

She looked at me dubiously, and by then we had reached the gipsies. She liked those, for she recognised who they were, and clapped her hands in glee. But when she got to my gipsy boy, she stopped, and the light went out of her eyes as she stood staring at him.

I kept very still. Was she just as mesmerised by the perfection of the figure as I was, or was there some other reason why she suddenly looked so stricken?

After what seemed an age, she said:

'I don't like him. Can we go?'

'Of course. Let me shew you the rest of the house. It's beautiful, and you'll love it as I do.'

And she did. She skipped from room to room, touching the graceful furniture with her long slender fingers, admiring the paintings, darting to a window now and then to look down at the gardens.

'There's something else I want you to see,' I said finally. 'We have to go into the garden to get there. Come along.'

Still happy and contented she followed me, holding her face up to the sun. When I drew her towards the door leading to the cellars, she stopped.

'Where are we going?'

'Just to see the cellars. There are a lot of them, and there's a wine store with hundreds of bottles.'

She hung back.

'I don't want to go down there.'

'Why ever not?' I pretended to laugh at her reluctance. 'You never know, we might find some more candies there too.'

At first I thought she would refuse to go through the door, but perhaps her sweet tooth made her change her mind. She wasn't smiling now as we walked through the dark passages, lit here and there by lanterns on the walls. All her happiness seemed to have fallen away from her, and when I looked at her eyes I could see the increasing fear in them. I knew then that I was growing closer to Cassie's riddle, although I hated what I was doing to poor Oriel.

Finally we reached the door with the padlock.

'Even I have never been in here,' I said, still watching her. 'Shall we try to open it and explore together?'

She cringed away from me, and then began that dreadful whimpering I had heard before.

'Oriel! It's all right. There's nothing to be afraid of. It's just another cellar, isn't it?'

'No! No!' She was crouched down on all fours now, pupils dilated, one hand stretching out as if to push the closed door away from her. 'No, no, I can't go in there . . . I won't! You can't make me! I won't go in there.'

Somehow I got her to her feet, and found that her body was as rigid as any of Cassie's waxworks. Then she pulled herself away from me and ran off.

I hurried after her, but she was already out of sight by the time I had closed the outer door behind me. I leaned against it for a while, thinking hard.

Oriel had shewn no reluctance to enter Steeple Court. She had obviously enjoyed the waxworks, with the exception of the gipsy boy, and had murmured with gratification when I had taken her from room to room, filled with Cassie's treasures of china, porcelain, silver and golden ornaments.

Only when we had gone into the cellars had Oriel's fear begun. She hadn't liked the large cellars very much, but it had not been until we reached the locked door that the real terror in her had bubbled to the surface. But why should Oriel Stewart be afraid of a cellar in Steeple Court? It was improbable that she had ever been inside the house before; she said she had not seen the waxworks. What

183

was it, then, about this door which had sent her flying from the place in stark panic?

I was determined to open that door and find out what was behind it, but then I looked at my fob-watch and saw that it was four-thirty. I had been with Oriel longer than I thought, and Chloe was coming to tea with me that day.

I hurried back to the house and changed my gown, apologising profusely when I found that Chloe was already waiting for me in the sitting-room.

'I'm so sorry,' I said as she proferred her cheek. 'I fell asleep on my bed. It must be the heat; do forgive me.'

'Of course, love, it doesn't matter, and I've only just arrived. You do look rather pale, Selina. Is anything wrong?'

'No, of course not.' I should have put a touch of rouge on my face. Trust Chloe to notice that all was not well. 'I'm fine.'

'David says you should have a holiday.' She sat down again, arranging the skirt of her green silk gown with an expert hand. 'He thinks you look peaky too.'

'I expect it is because of the accident I had on the stairs, to say nothing of that intruder who attacked me, but I'm really quite well now.'

I wished Jessie would hurry up and bring

in the tray, because I wanted to be done with the subject of my health and the holiday all my friends thought I should take.

'Yes, you've had a bad time.' Chloe drew off her gloves. 'But you know it's more likely that you've made yourself poorly by worrying over that old letter from your aunt.' She shook a finger at me. 'Such a silly girl, Selina. Why, it was years ago that she wrote it; you said so yourself. Besides, not a soul has any idea what she meant. Nothing could have happened, or at least one of the people here would have known about it, yet you're still asking questions. Do put it out of your mind, or you really will make yourself ill.'

'I've already done so,' I lied, and sighed with relief as Jessie appeared, followed by Nell with the tea-kettle. 'I was silly, as you say, but it's all over and done with now.'

Chloe said no more until the maids had gone. Then she gave me a searching look.

'Rumour tells me that Anthony is trying to persuade you to go to Venice? Is that true?'

'Did he tell you that?'

'No, I heard it from someone else, but I can't think who it was. I can't imagine Anthony going away. He always said he would never leave the Moors. Will you go?'

'I doubt it. Do have one of these sandwiches.'

She took one, nodding her thanks.

'Do you know, when I was coming up the drive I could have sworn I saw Oriel Stewart running away from the house. Has she been here?'

I took a careful sip of tea.

'Oriel? Why, no, I haven't seen her. Of course, she could have been in the grounds without my knowledge. She wanders about so much.'

I thought my ability to lie with conviction was getting better each time I practised it, for Chloe seemed to accept what I said without suspicion.

'It still seems odd to me,' I went on, 'that Marcus Tarrant allows her so much freedom. Since he is so protective in some ways, it is remarkable that she could vanish for two days without anyone finding her. Do you know where she could have gone, Chloe?'

'I?' Chloe's violet eyes turned to me in surprise. 'No, of course not. How could I know what the girl gets up to?'

'Well, you used to play together when you were children, didn't you? I had assumed you did, anyway. Didn't you have some special place to hide? Most children do.'

Chloe went back to her sandwich.

'We did play together, of course, Oriel, Anthony, David and I. Oriel was always afraid of everything though, and we often left her behind because she was such a cry-baby. As to somewhere special to hide . . . there was a disused mill about half a mile away from here which we used to go to when we could get away from our respective governesses. It's been pulled down now, for it wasn't safe.' She gave a slight laugh. 'We used to take great pains in escaping from the hand of authority and getting to that mill. Last one there had to pay a fine, or do something which the others told him or her to do.'

'What sort of things?'

'Oh you know, the kind of awful things children dream up. Once we made Oriel eat a whole handful of dirt. I think it made her ill for a week, but we didn't care. Then, when I was last, the boys said I must take off all my clothes and cross the stream down there.'

'Chloe! You didn't do it, did you?'

'Of course.' Her face was alight with mischief. 'I had a good body, even at that age, and I wasn't ashamed to shew it off, not even in front of David and Anthony. Oh dear, have I shocked you?'

'Of course not.' This time I was speaking the truth, for I could imagine Chloe Oldfield capable of accepting any challenge. 'You must have had a lovely time together; you,

187

Anthony, David and Oriel.'

'It was all right.' She raised her shoulders negligently. 'I would rather Marcus had been there too, but he would never have anything to do with us.'

'Why not?'

'I don't know. Perhaps his parents wouldn't let him.' The curling lashes half-covered her eyes. 'He was handsome even as a boy, but when he came down from Oxford, I thought him devastating. Do you like him, Selina?'

More lies as I re-filled her cup.

'Not particularly, and he doesn't like me either.'

'I can't think why. I love you.'

'Thank you, Chloe.' I coloured slightly, still unused to people expressing their emotions quite so openly. 'And you know that I'm very fond of you too.'

'What a pity we can't make others love us, isn't it?' She sighed as she took a macaroon from the plate I was holding out to her. 'If we could, I would make Marcus love me, and get rid of that stupid girl. Oh, Selina, why can't he see how senseless it is to try to keep her here? Why can't he put her away, and then he might see me properly?'

It was a cry from the heart, but I didn't know how to answer it, or how to help Chloe, for that matter.

'Is it still said that he will marry her?'

'The rumour hasn't died down, although whether or not it's true, I don't know. He really has no need to marry her, has he?'

I knew exactly what she meant, for the same reprehensible thought had occurred to me in the past, but I feigned ignorance of her innuendo.

'Well no, of course not. He can simply remain her guardian.'

Chloe's smile was derisive.

'I often wonder if you are as naïve as you would have us all believe. Sometimes you seem as innocent as Oriel herself.'

'And on other occasions?' I kept my voice even. 'What about the other times?'

She laughed.

'It is said that still waters run deep. Now and then, I wonder if your waters are not as deep as those in the old well in your garden.'

'I don't think so,' I said finally. 'I think your first assessment is probably right. Remember, I led a very sheltered life in India.'

'On a military post?'

'Of which my father was the commanding officer.' My smile was sweet and untroubled. 'I was always treated with the very greatest of respect.'

189

'I'm sure you were. Ah well, I must go.'

She rose and looked at me silently until I thought she must have seen the blush rise in my cheeks.

'Think about that holiday,' she said at last. 'A change is good for everyone.'

As I rang for Jessie, I forebore to remind Chloe that I had only been in Leyden for a short time, and was hardly in need of a change of scene yet. It seemed that everyone was anxious for me to go away. Perhaps the worry Anthony had seen in me, and had transferred so expertly to canvas, was more obvious than I had realised.

When Chloe had gone, I sat down to make a decision. Should I go to the cellars now, or later when everyone was asleep? In the end I chose the latter course, for it would be dark down there whatever the hour, and there was less likelihood of anyone hearing me if they were all in bed.

I hated the very thought of it, but I knew it had to be done. I had to find out why Oriel Stewart was terrified of that closed door, and what lay behind it. There was only one way to do this, and that was to go and look.

9

At one o'clock I went down to the cellars. The mind is a strange thing, and, as David had said, it can play many tricks. Although the small lanterns were always kept burning in the storage rooms, the place felt quite different now that night had fallen. It was just like the gallery all over again.

Earlier that day, when I had been down there with Oriel, I had known that all I had to do to reach blessed daylight was to run up a few stairs. Now there was darkness both inside and out.

As I passed the wood-cellar I noticed a thin metal rod which I picked up. It would help me to shift that stubborn padlock. By the wine-cellar I stopped again.

Suppose there was something behind that door which shouldn't be there? What was I going to do about it? There was no Gertie from whom to seek advice, and I was not sure who else in Leyden, I could really trust. Cassie hadn't trusted anyone, so how could I?

For the life of me I couldn't think whom it was that my aunt had feared. Everyone in the village and the surrounding houses were so normal and affable, especially my new friends. David, rather staid, but a dear for all that. Anthony, a trifle unconventional, perhaps, but warm and almost tender at times. Chloe, a gay companion and loving friend, only really hurtful when she thought about the man she loved and could never have. Oriel, incapable of anything which would harm another. Surely Cassie couldn't have been frightened of the Misses Fanshawe, the colonel and his wife, or any of the simple village folk, yet who was there left?

There was only one person I knew who might instil that kind of fear. I leaned against the wall for a second and closed my eyes. I didn't want it to be Marcus Tarrant, but it was hard to get away from the thought that he was the most likely suspect.

The fact that he had agreed with the *bibi*'s view that Gertie was dead, by no means meant that he hadn't killed her. He had been furious with me for upsetting Oriel, and had said bluntly that he would not use words again. Despite his vehement denial had he kept his promise and come through my bedroom window that night?

But how could Marcus be involved with Cassie's problem of so many years ago? At the relevant time he was up at Oxford. I bit my lip.

But not, of course, in the long vacation. Marcus would have come back to Leyden then.

It was no good dwelling on vague possibilities, and so I went along the passage and started work on the door at the far end. It took time, but finally I managed to wrench off the padlock. I paused once more, not liking the sound the wood made as it swung inwards, very reluctant to enter the black hole yawning in front of me.

I gripped my lamp hard, and kept the rod with me, just in case. It was a fairly large room, and once inside I lit a rusty lantern which was hanging on the wall, which gave a grudging light. There wasn't much there; a few packing cases and boxes, and on one side a large tin trunk.

I stood and gazed at if for a long while. I knew at once that this was what I was looking for; instinct told me so, yet it was several minutes before I could cross the floor towards it. I heard a sudden scuffle and saw a large grey rat darting to its hole.

I shuddered, for I hated rats, finally taking the last few steps towards the trunk. I didn't want to look inside it, but I knew that I had to. I couldn't just stand there, shivering with cold and dread.

The lid was firmly fastened; quite air-tight. It took me at least five minutes of hard banging with my rod to shift it, but finally I succeeded.

When I opened it up, the metal bar fell from my nerveless fingers, clattering to the floor. I picked up the lamp again, almost overcome by a smell so frightful that I thought I was going to faint. I forced myself to raise the light so that I could see more clearly the contents of that dreadful trunk. Then the lid slammed down, and I staggered into the corner and was violently sick.

It was the remains of a boy; that much I knew. Somehow, despite the condition of what was left of him, he reminded me of the gipsy in the gallery. I had no idea why, because the wax model was a thing of sheer beauty, whilst the object in the trunk had crawled out of a nightmare.

I knew I had to get out of that cellar before I lost consciousness. The air was filled with an appalling odour, and my head was swimming. If I collapsed on the floor in here, heaven knows whether I should ever wake again.

I backed away, ready to run, when I heard the slight sound behind me. I turned quickly,

194

thinking that perhaps Ben Goodbody or Tom Greenlaw, who lived in cottages near to the outhouses, had heard the noise I had been making.

But it wasn't the reassuring bulk of the gardener or coachman that I saw, but a glimpse of grey hair, neatly dressed, a dainty lace scarf at the neck, and broad shoulders under a lilac-coloured gown.

I could feel my flesh creep. The figure seemed to me to be a shade more ghastly than the thing in the trunk, for at least that was still, whereas the new arrival was moving, and had taken a step towards me.

I didn't believe it, but I said it nevertheless. 'Aunt Cassie?'

It was such a feeble quaver that I repeated it, to make sure that she had heard me.

'Aunt Cassie, is that you? But it can't be! You're dead. I went to your funeral, and saw your grave. It can't be . . . '

From its shadowed position the figure gave a quiet and rather muffled laugh.

'So you did, my dear, but, if you recall, you saw me in the gallery too, after the funeral.'

'I believed that I had dreamt it. I knew you were dead, and so I thought that in the darkness . . . '

'No, it wasn't a dream. I was there.'

'But how could you have been? Dr. Stannard told me that you had died of a heart attack.'

'Such a good boy, David. Always so helpful.'

I hung on to a packing case, lest my knees gave way from under me, leaving me prey to this preposterous apparition.

'But I don't understand. Why should you pretend to be dead?'

'I had my reasons.'

The words were still no more than a whisper and not very clear. Even in the midst of my terror, I was surprised, for I had always imagined Cassie would have a firm and decisive voice.

'I see.' I moistened my dry lips. 'Was it because of what you said in your letter to me?'

'Letter? You mean the one I sent to you when you were a child?'

'No, the one you sent to Grey's Hotel in London last month. Surely you can't have forgotten it? You were so desperate that I should come and see you, so that you could talk to me. You said you couldn't trust anyone but me. You must remember that!'

'Oh yes, that letter. Forgive me, my memory is not good these days. I grow old.'

A strange suspicion was beginning to mingle with my fear.

'You mean you were afraid for your life, and that David Stannard helped you by pretending that you had died, so that you could stay hidden until I arrived? But if you trusted him that much, why didn't you tell him what was worrying you, and why, if you couldn't do that, have you not spoken to me before? I have been here some weeks.'

'All in good time. I have been waiting for the right opportunity.'

'And this is it?' I was incredulous. 'Here, in this place? Do you know what is in there?' I pointed to the trunk. 'And how did you know I had come down to the cellars?'

'I was watching you with Oriel this afternoon. I have kept an eye on you ever since you arrived, and Isa has just told me that you left your bedroom some half hour ago. I guessed you would come here.'

'Isa is aware that you're still alive?' It was another small shock. 'Does anyone else know?'

'No, but I had to tell her, because someone had to get me food and help me to conceal myself. But only she and David realise that I am not buried out there in the churchyard.'

'I still don't understand why you have waited so long to talk to me. Why . . . '

'In a moment.' The figure moved another step nearer. 'Isa tells me that you have one of the emeralds. Where did you find it?'

'But you know.' Again the fleeting doubt, crossing my mind like a sudden gust of wind. 'Why do you ask me that? It was you, surely, who stuck them on the costumes of the waxworks amongst the pieces of paste. Does Isa know you did that?'

'Ah . . . of course . . . the costumes. No, Isa doesn't know.'

'But why did you do it? Why didn't you put them in the bank if you weren't going to wear them?'

'I liked to look at them now and then, but if I had kept them all together, someone might have stolen them. I have an enemy, you see.'

'Yes, I supposed that by the way you wrote. Aunt Cassie, what is this thing you have not spoken of for so many years?'

My query was ignored; the only response another question.

'What made you come down here to-day? Why did you bring Oriel into the cellars?'

'Because of the clue you gave me in the other note you left. Also I have felt for a long time that Oriel knew what happened all those years ago. When she saw the door of this cellar, I was certain of it.'

'Note? What note?'

The whisper was sharper now, and so were my suspicions.

'The one in the musical box, of course. Don't you recall that either? You said: 'Look to the heights for that which is beautiful.' That's why I had another look round the gallery, for that is the highest part of the house. It was then that I found the emerald and understood what you meant. You also said: 'and look to the depths for that which is ugly and evil.' I did that too, and found this . . . this thing in the trunk. Your last words puzzled me though.'

I was trying to see Cassie's face more clearly, but she was still too far away for the faint light to shew more than a pale oval blur.

'What did you mean when you said: 'for the rest, ask Henry?' Who is Henry?'

'Henry?' There was real uncertainty in the husky voice now. 'Shew me the note.'

'I haven't got it with me. Who is he?'

'Have you spoken to anyone else about this?'

'No.'

'Sensible girl. Always wise to keep such things to yourself. What about the emerald?

Does anyone know you have found it, or where?'

'No.'

'Better still.'

'Please, Cassie, we can't stay down here all night. Tell me about the matter which . . . '

'Yes, yes, soon.'

'And what about that . . . that thing over there? Who was he, and what happened to him? Is that part of what you have been hiding?'

'Oh no, he was just a tinker's brat from the camp outside my garden.'

I stood very still, knuckles bone-white as I clutched at the packing case. Cassie, who had loved the Romanies; watched them; sketched them; dressed them; and written about them. Cassie, who now called the horror behind me a tinker's brat.

'You're not Cassie, I said finally, my voice unsteady as I strained my eyes again in a desperate effort to see who it was. 'You knew nothing of the letter which I received in London until I told you about it just now. You didn't know where the jewels were either, did you?'

'Of course I'm Cassie, and certainly I remember the letter, and where I hid my gems for safe-keeping. You're being silly, child.'

The whisper was harsher, and now I wasn't sure whether it was a man or a woman in the lilac gown.

'I don't think so. I might have believed in your lapses of memory, unlikely though they were, but nothing would ever convince me that my aunt would refer to a pure Romany as a tinker. She loved the Romanies, you see, and she knew all about them. A Romany and a tinker are very different things. She knew that, but you didn't. Who are you? Why are you doing these things? Was it you who killed my maid, Gertrude, and came into my room and beat me? If so, in God's name, why?'

'I'm your aunt, of course, who else could I be? You're distraught, that's what it is. I'll come closer so that you can see for yourself.'

The figure began to advance, passing under the dim lantern which hung on a piece of wood projecting from the wall. I saw its rough end catch in the grey hair, expecting the unknown person to free it with one hand and come on, but the hands didn't move.

Then, as I watched, I could see the hair begin to slip. I opened my mouth, but no sounds came, for it was not only the hair which was shifting in such a macabre fashion; the whole of the head was tilting sideways as it started to detach itself from the body.

Then I did scream.

'Oh my God! No! No! Your head is falling off! What sort of creature are you? Get away from me . . . get away from me . . . for pity's sake! Your head . . . your head is coming off . . . oh no!'

I fled, but in my panic I did not see the round metal rod. I felt my feet giving way under me, grabbing at empty air as I went down, striking my head on the side of the trunk as I slid quietly into oblivion.

★ ★ ★

When I awoke twenty-four hours later, it was to find that I was in my own bed, suffering from a mild concussion. A doctor, whom I had never seen before, was shutting his bag and saying firmly:

'If you insist on staying, Sir Marcus, it can only be for a short time. Miss Rochford must rest.'

I turned my head, regretting it at once as fresh hammers began to beat on my skull. But there was Marcus, sitting by my side, watching me with a smile which made my heart turn over.

When he had assured the doctor that he would do nothing to upset me, we were left alone, and I said weakly:

202

'What happened? How long have I been in bed?'

'Not long, and you'll soon be fit again.' He gave a slight laugh. 'Fortunately, you are a blockhead, as I have said on several occasions, and so you have sustained no lasting injuries.'

I hadn't heard him laugh before; it was a wonderful sound.

'I expect you want to know why I'm here.' He looked at me soberly, the flash of humour gone. 'Since we have so little time, perhaps I'd better tell you what happened.'

'Yes, please.'

I tried to sit up, but was gently and firmly pushed back against the pillows. Accepting this gesture without argument, I said quickly:

'The last thing I recall was being in the cellar.' I could feel the remembered chill crawling over me again. 'There was someone there. She . . . or he . . . I'm not sure which, said that they were Aunt Cassie, but I didn't believe them.'

I saw that my hands were shaking against the whiteness of the sheet.

'Then . . . then . . . their head began to fall off. I know you'll think I'm really mad now, but that's what happened. Their head came off. Then there was a trunk.' I swallowed hard. 'I looked inside it and I found . . . I saw . . . ' I closed my eyes unable to describe what the passing years had done to the body of the boy. 'And . . . the smell . . . that terrible smell . . . '

Suddenly Marcus's hands were over mine, holding them tightly until I stopped trembling.

'I know, I know, but let me go on.'

'Yes, of course, I'm sorry. I won't interrupt again, but just tell me this. Was it Aunt Cassie?'

'No, my dear, it wasn't. Cassie Van Doren died of a heart attack when Stannard said she did. She's safely in her grave.'

'Then . . . '

'Now we go back to the start of this horrible affair.' Marcus had lines round the corners of his mouth which I hadn't noticed before, and he was finding it difficult to begin. Finally he said: 'I know the whole story now, for while you have been lying here, I have been asking questions, finding evidence, and getting confessions, which explain all that has mystified you, and me too, incidentally.'

There was another pause, and I could not take my eyes off his face.

'It began fifteen years ago, when four children dared each other to leave their homes one dark night and meet in your aunt's garden. It was June; a hot summer like this one. There were two boys aged fifteen and thirteen; two girls of eleven and five respectively. The five-year-old didn't want to go, but the others threatened her until she accepted the dare.'

'Oriel.' I murmured it half under my breath.

'That's right, Oriel. A small, nervous, highly-strung little thing, who was constantly exposed to the vicious bullying of the other three.'

I wanted to ask who the others were, but Marcus was speaking again.

'When they got to their rendezvous, it seems they met a gipsy boy who had sneaked into the garden from the camp nearby. There was a quarrel, for the two boys and the other girl had no time for what they described as a dirty tinker. The boy was tough, however, and he was nearly winning the fight which ensued, when the girl hit him over the head with a stone. She wasn't a robust child, but she had a wiry strength which was almost demoniacal when she was aroused.

'When they looked at the gipsy again, they found he was dead. They each had a lamp with them, and with the aid of these they made their way to the outer door of your aunt's cellar, and put the body in a trunk they found below.

'They had to carry Oriel home, for when

they had finished their job, they found she was in such a condition that she was incapable of walking or of coherent speech. As you know, she never recovered her senses, and from that night onwards has been as she was then; like a child of five. The others watched her closely for a day or two, but it was clear that she had no memory of what had happened, and they were satisfied that she could never speak of what had taken place.

'What they did not realise, however, was that they had been seen by someone else. Your aunt could not sleep that night, and she'd been wandering about the house. She was over on that side of the building when she heard the noise and looked out of a window very close to where the fight took place. By the light of the lamps, she saw all that happened. She had sharp eyesight, for she even saw the dead boy's face well enough to make a sketch of it.

'She was paralysed for a while, because she knew the children, one particularly well. The next morning she went quietly down to the cellars and eventually found the room you were in to-night, saw the trunk, and knew what they had done with the body. She got hold of a padlock and secured the room, and then threw the key away.

'For three days she struggled with her conscience, and prayed for guidance. Her duty was obvious, but they were only children, and one was her nephew.'

'Anthony! Oh, but he wouldn't . . . '

'The other two were David Stannard and Chloe Oldfield. Chloe was always their leader.' Marcus's mouth was a tight line. 'In the end, Cassie decided to say nothing, but for the rest of her life she lived with that terrible knowledge.

'For several years she managed to exist normally, although she always tried to avoid the children, pretending she didn't approve of Anthony because of his father. But as she got older, she started to draw more and more inside herself. I think her dread began to increase when the children grew up. They had killed once; she knew they would not hesitate to kill again. I think that is why her waxworks were so important to her. It was an outlet for her energies, and an escape. When she was working on the costumes, she could almost forget what was buried in her heart. Then at last she got Mr. Porter to make her gipsy boy. She knew it was a risk, because one of the three could easily have gone to the gallery, noticed the figure, and realised that Cassie might have seen them with him that night. She took the chance because by then she knew she hadn't much longer to live, and somehow she felt it was right that the boy shouldn't be entirely forgotten. The irony of it was that none of the three children even noticed the Romany's face; they were too busy moving his body. Only Cassie had seen it, and remembered it.

'When Chloe and the others knew you were coming, they were not particularly concerned, for Cassie had died a natural death and there was no reason for you to ask questions. But when you began talking about a note which you had received from your aunt years before, mentioning an incident which had clearly upset her very much, they began to grow cautious.

'At first they thought you would forget the subject after being assured that nothing had happened. Then they began to see what kind of girl you were; determined, and not one to give up easily, and you were asking too many people too many questions.

'They decided the simplest thing to do was to frighten you away from Steeple Court; only later did they realise they would have to kill you to save themselves.

'Knowing how Isa doted on Anthony, they got her to help them, promising her that once you had left, he would be able to live at Steeple Court in grand style. At that stage,

Isa was only too glad to assist. She gave them keys to the front door, the gallery, and the entrance to the back stairs. She also helped them to make a wig and a wax model of Cassie's face and neck. They fixed those on to a kind of harness, which Chloe wore when she appeared in the gallery, and in the cellars, so that she looked much taller. There were holes in the neck behind the scarf, so that she could breathe and speak. The reason for her appearance to-night was that they didn't know where you had found the emerald. Chloe knew you would never tell her, but if she could convince you that she was Cassie, there was no reason for you not to discuss the matter with your aunt, as indeed you did.

'Anthony Sewall may not have shewn his bitter resentment at being cut out of the Will, but the corrosive fury was there right enough. He wanted those jewels, and Chloe intended to have her share of them too.'

'So it was Chloe?' Something painful squeezed my heart. Chloe wasn't the loving, light-hearted girl I had thought her to be at all. She had taken the Romany boy's life without compunction, hiding her true self behind a mask of gaiety. 'What was she going to do with me?'

'Once you had told her where the gems

209

were, she was going to kill you and leave you there with the gipsy boy. Anthony would go to Venice, and people would have been told that you had gone with him.'

Marcus's voice was curt.

'When I got there, she had torn off the false head which had caught on that piece of wood, and she had a knife in her hand.'

'Oh God!' I kept my tears to myself, for there was much more I wanted to know. 'How did you know we were in the cellars?'

'Oriel got home that night about ten o'clock. She was in a terrible state, much worse than usual, and I knew then that something was seriously wrong. I had guessed for a long time that all was not well, but I didn't know what was going on. I thought your maid had been murdered, and when you were attacked I was sure things were coming to a climax.'

'Who . . . who did that? Who beat me?'

'Your precious cousin, Sewall. When I saw the condition you were in the next morning, I hardly knew how to control myself. I have never been so angry in my life, but if I had shewn how I felt, it would have made whoever was responsible more wary. I didn't want that, much as I needed to comfort you. You must have thought me utterly without feeling.'

'Anthony!' I felt a lump in my throat. 'Oh no, it couldn't have been.'

Anthony who had painted me with such skill; who had kissed me with something near to passion; who had called me his lovely coz, and had wanted to take me away with him.

'It was Sewall right enough. he did it partly to throw suspicion on me, in view of my well-publicized threats, partly to keep up the good work of frightening you out of Leyden, but mostly because Chloe told him to. He was quite happy to comply with her order, for he hated you because you got Cassie's fortune and he got nothing.'

Anthony had hated me that much? Still, I could hardly believe it. Not for one second had he shewn anything but affection for me, and I felt hollow inside, aching with the shock. I glanced at Marcus. He looked bleak, hands locked together as if he would like to have had Anthony's neck between them.

'When Oriel came home, I started to question her. I kept on and on and on until at last I broke down the barriers of years. When she disappeared for those two days, Chloe and the others had taken her, and threatened her with dire consequences if she were to open her mouth. They need not have troubled themselves then, for she had no idea what they were talking about, and by the time she got home again she had no recollection of where she had been. But I made her remember.'

He looked almost grey.

'When I first arrived here to-night, I met Isa Hedley coming up from the cellars. She was almost demented. Gradually, she had become more and more frightened of Chloe and the others, sure that it was not just Anthony's well-being which was at stake. She followed Chloe downstairs and heard most of what was said, including the place where Cassie had hidden the jewels. It was she, of course, who told me about the wax head, and the fact that you had found the emerald. She had watched through the open door of your room as you examined the stone, but she didn't know where you had found it until to-night. She told Chloe about the emerald, but she didn't mention to her the note which she gave to me. She was snooping through your bureau when she discovered that, but by then she was petrified of Chloe and Anthony, and didn't want to know what was ugly and evil in the basement. Nevertheless, in the end she couldn't help herself, and she went after Chloe, praise be to God.'

'But how do you know that Cassie saw the children, if they didn't know it themselves?'

Marcus's drawn look lightened fractionally.

'I asked Henry, of course, as Cassie suggested.'

'Henry?' I frowned. 'Oh yes, of course, but who on earth *is* Henry?'

'Henry VIII, and in his sleeve I found that Cassie had taken a chance after all and written down everything which she was going to tell you. She had a premonition that she wouldn't live long enough to see you, and so she left this letter.'

Marcus drew it from his pocket and laid it on the bed.

'Read it when you are better. Since by then I knew where Cassie had concealed the jewellery, it wasn't too difficult to guess what she meant by 'ask Henry'. I think she was beginning to suspect Isa, hence the caution.

'The thing which appalled your aunt most of all was not that the children had killed the gipsy, but that they were totally uncaring that they had done so, either then, or later. Amoral hardly described them. Cassie thought them scarcely human; to her they were monsters. She watched them year by year, living happy, normal lives as if nothing had happened. It seemed to her worse when they became adults, and Stannard went off to study medicine, Sewall became an artist, and Chloe a beautiful young woman full of laughter and fun. It was as if the whole thing had been a bad dream, but she knew it wasn't, and she realised that if ever she gave herself away, it would be the end of her.

'When old Dr. Pemberton retired, and Stannard returned to take over his practice, Cassie was numb.

Marcus picked up the letter again.

'She says: 'I dreaded having David as my doctor, but what could I do? Everyone else in Leyden had accepted him as their physician, and if I had refused, he might have wondered why. But, oh, how I hated the feel of his hands on me.' '

'Oh, Cassie! Cassie!' The tears were running down my cheeks. 'Why didn't you write before? Why didn't you tell me in your letters what was happening?'

'Because you were too far away, and Cassie Van Doren was a brave woman. She didn't want you upset, and so she stuck it out until she knew you were home.'

Marcus raised his head.

'All three of them have made full confessions: indeed, Chloe seemed to take a delight in giving us every last gruesome detail, once she knew the game was up. She watched you take Oriel to the cellars, and guessed you would return later when she saw Oriel run off in fear. That night, when Isa told her you'd left your room, Chloe put on her disguise and followed you.'

'What about my poor Gertie? Is she dead?'

'I'm afraid so.' He was very gentle. 'You see, Isa overheard her mention to you that she had seen someone in the corridor the night before. She didn't have time to tell you that it was Chloe, for Jessie Trent called you away. Isa told Chloe at once, and was sent back to Gertrude with a message saying that you wanted her in the gardens, where you were walking with Stannard. Naturally, Gertie went, and that's when they took her. Chloe has obligingly told us in which ditch to look for her body. Isa got hold of a sample of Gertie's writing, so that the two notes you received would be convincing, although she had no idea at that time that Gertie had been killed. Anthony is as gifted with a pen as with a paintbrush. He is no mean forger.'

'I can't bear it,' I said in a whisper. 'She was so much more than a maid. She'd been with me almost all my life, and I loved her.'

'I know, I know, but don't grieve, for that's the last thing Gertie would have wanted. At least we've brought her killers to book.'

'Did Chloe and the others have anything to do with those odd things which happened in the servants' quarters? I mean the flying saucepan, and the bell-ringing.'

215

'Indeed they did. First, they paid Dorcas's parents to take her away from here, and then they produced Bethia Tudball. Bethia, despite her tender years, has already had four positions and been dismissed from them all for the same reason. Wherever she went, similar things occurred. No one quite knows why some people have these powers, but it is recognized that certain girls, particularly of Bethia's age, can cause such phenomena. Chloe knew all about Bethia, and that was their first attempt to scare you.'

'I think the staff was more frightened than I was.'

'Yes, and when that didn't work, they dared you to spend fifteen minutes in the gallery at night. Chloe let you catch a glimpse of her dressed as Cassie, whilst Isa, slipping in from the back stairs, turned a figure round in the hope that you would think it had moved of its own volition.'

I gave a shaky laugh.

'I almost did believe it.'

'The noises you heard at night were Chloe and the others searching for the jewels, which Sewall was so determined to have. They used the keys Isa had given them. That was how Gertie saw Chloe in the corridor.'

'And when I fell downstairs?'

Marcus's face was like thunder.

'A black cord across the stairs, put there, and later removed by, Isa Hedley, on Chloe's instructions. Isa made sufficient noise to awaken you, again on Chloe's orders. She was too frightened of Chloe by then to disobey.'

'I still can't quite believe it.' I lay back and shut my eyes. 'They were all so . . . well . . . ordinary and kind, just like anyone else. They seemed to have an affection for me, and at times I thought Anthony was in love with me.'

'Did you indeed?'

Marcus's tone was decidedly encouraging.

'Did Anthony tell you that he had asked me for money? He said he had debts of some two thousand, but I gave him five thousand, for I thought he should have some of Cassie's fortune.'

'Yes, he told me, and laughed about it. It was true enough that he had debts, but he thought you a fool to part with anything, let alone five thousand.'

I swallowed again, trying to turn away from the subject of Anthony.

'And poor Oriel . . . '

'She was guiltless.' Marcus's voice was full of pain. 'She was dragged around after the others when she was a child, simply because they wanted someone weak and helpless to

217

torment. She had no part in the killing of the gipsy, but it was she who paid the greatest price.'

'How is she now?'

'Mad.'

'Mad? You mean she's worse than . . . '

'I mean mad; just that.' Marcus's voice was lower still. 'I forced her to remember things buried so deeply in her mind, that when I dragged them to the surface she cracked completely. They have taken her away, and I can still hear her screams. I think I shall hear them for the rest of my life.'

It was my turn to comfort.

'Marcus, don't . . . please don't. It wasn't your fault. You had to find out what was wrong.'

'Yes, I did, but once again it is Oriel who has paid the price.'

'You loved her, didn't you?'

'Very much. She was the only sister I had.'

'Chloe thought you were going to marry her.'

'If she did, she was a fool, for there was never any question of that.' He glanced at me 'But it wasn't only Oriel of whom Chloe was jealous, whatever she may have said to you. I'm afraid I am much to

218

blame for the viciousness of that attack on you.'

'Oh? How could you possibly be responsible?'

'Because one day not long before, I had told Chloe that I thought you were a hard-hearted shrew, with no manners and even less sense, but that you were the most beautiful woman I had ever seen. Chloe was in love with me. I knew that, although I did not return her feelings. She ignored my strictures about you, but she remembered the rest. She knew me better than I knew myself, and I suspect that she was aware of the exact moment when I stopped disliking you and began to love you. That is why she told Anthony to thrash you in that way. It was sheer, unadulterated malice.'

I turned my head, and he saw the look on my face.

'You hadn't guessed?' He was faintly amused. 'You still thought that I disliked you?'

'Well . . . yes I did.' I blushed as I made my confession. 'I only knew that I loved you. I didn't think that . . . '

'Then you were less perceptive than Chloe.'

'What will happen to her?'

'Chloe? She'll stand trial for murder with the others.'

'They won't . . . they won't hang her, will they?'

'I have no idea, but, if they do, Chloe is the sort of woman who will go to the scaffold laughing. She's cold-blooded, savage, inhuman and vindictive, but she is not a coward.'

'I would hate to think . . . '

'Forget her.' Marcus was firm. 'What are you going to do now?'

I looked at him doubtfully.

'Well, I suppose I'll stay here and look after Cassie's children, as she asked me to do. Does she say in the letter why she never mentioned the gallery to me?'

'Yes, it was to be a surprise for you. She thought, of course, that she would be alive to shew it to you herself. In this letter, written after the one she sent to you in London, she says she wishes she had told you all about it before. She knew by then that she would never have the chance of introducing you to her children.'

'I see. Poor Cassie.'

'If you insist on staying to look after the gallery, so be it, but when the time comes for you to look after your own children, someone else will have to wield a feather duster over those waxworks.'

'My own children! I'm not even married.'

'Well, we've hardly had time to make the arrangements, have we, and because you are somewhat slow-witted, you have only just discovered who your husband is to be.'

He was laughing at me, but I didn't care. I knew that I ought to make some shy, maidenly protest, but it hardly seemed worth the effort. Instead, I stretched out my hand and took his.

'Marcus, are you sure?'

He didn't bother to answer me, and when the doctor returned and found me in Marcus's arms he was furious, sending Marcus packing at once. It didn't matter though, for I would soon be up and about again and, after all, Marcus and I had the rest of our lives before us.

★ ★ ★

Chloe Oldfield did not hang, for the simple reason that she never came to trial, but her end was far worse than anything civilized law could devise.

When the police had concluded their enquiries, they set out for York, Anthony and David in one carriage, Chloe and Isa in another. Five miles out of Leyden the vehicle in which Chloe was travelling was lagging behind; the other had raced on round the bend and was out of sight.

Afterwards, the guards said they couldn't really tell what had happened; it was all over so quickly. A large band of Romanies had come riding up at high speed, and in a matter or minutes the coach was overturned, its wheels ripped off, its bodywork hacked to pieces.

When the dazed and injured constables finally got to their feet, there wasn't a gipsy in sight, but what they did see was a heap of crumpled green silk some distance away. As they approached it, they had heard the screams of the older woman, whose eyes were wild and half-mad. Then they looked down at their other prisoner, remembering well enough the fashionable gown, but the face was unrecognisable for it had been smashed to pulp by a heavy stone which still lay by the woman's side.

How the Romanies had found out so quickly that Chloe had been arrested and had gaily and unrepentantly confessed to the killing of the gipsy boy, no one will ever know. The Romanies had their own way of discovering these things, which they kept to themselves.

'Normally peaceable beings,' Cassie had written, 'but with long memories, and who will fight to defend themselves. The death of one member of the family is a tragedy for them all.'

She had been right. The Romanies had had long memories and they had been patient too. It wasn't too difficult to see what had happened. The *bibi* had told me that they were waiting for something, and now I guessed what it was.

Fifteen years before, on their first visit to Leyden, one of their children had disappeared when they were camping outside Cassie's grounds. The child whom Chloe and the others called a dirty tinker.

When he didn't return, they finally went on their way, but they didn't forget him. Each year they made a pilgrimage to Leyden, sure that the boy had not merely run off, but that someone in the village or round about had made away with him. Probably he had been a loving child, who would never willingly have deserted his family, and so they had waited, certain that one day they would discover who had been responsible, and where his body lay.

They had not acted hastily, for they would never hurt the innocent, but from the moment that they had learned the truth, and summoned the rest of their tribe, there was never any doubt as to the end of Chloe Oldfield.

We do hope that you have enjoyed reading this large print book.

Did you know that all of our titles are available for purchase?

We publish a wide range of high quality large print books including:
Romances, Mysteries, Classics, General Fiction, Non Fiction and Westerns.

Special interest titles available in large print are:
The Little Oxford Dictionary
Music Book
Song Book
Hymn Book
Service Book

Also available from us courtesy of Oxford University Press:
Young Readers' Dictionary
(large print edition)
Young Readers' Thesaurus
(large print edition)

For further information or a free brochure, please contact us at:
Ulverscroft Large Print Books Ltd.,
The Green, Bradgate Road, Anstey,
Leicester, LE7 7FU, England.
Tel: (00 44) 0116 236 4325
Fax: (00 44) 0116 234 0205